DOCTOR WHO AND THE DESTINY OF THE DALEKS

GW00392443

DOCTOR WHO AND THE DESTINY OF THE DALEKS

Based on the BBC television serial by Terry Nation by arrangement with the British Broadcasting Corporation

TERRANCE DICKS

A TARGET BOOK
published by
the Paperback Division of
W. H. ALLEN & CO. LTD

A Target Book
Published in 1979
by the Paperback Division of W. H. Allen & Co. Ltd
A Howard & Wyndham Company
44 Hill Street, London W1X 8LB

Copyright © 1979 by Terrance Dicks, Lynsted Park Enterprises Ltd.
'Doctor Who' series copyright © 1979 by the
British Broadcasting Corporation
Daleks created by Terry Nation

Reprinted 1981

Reproduced, printed and bound in Great Britain by
Hazell Watson & Viney Ltd, Aylesbury, Bucks

ISBN 0 426 20096 9

Contents

1

The Dead City

Through the vortex, that mysterious region where time and space are one, sped a police box that was not a police box at all. It was, in fact, a highly sophisticated space/time ship called the TARDIS, a name taken from its initials, Time and Relative Dimensions in Space.

Inside its impossibly large control room (for the TARDIS was dimensionally transcendental) was a many-sided central console. Beside it a very tall man with a shock of curly hair was making minute adjustments to the larynx of a robot dog.

The robot dog was called K9, and the man trying to repair it was that mysterious traveller in time and space known as the Doctor. He wore loose, comfortable clothing, topped off with a broad-brimmed floppy soft hat, and an incredibly long multi-coloured scarf. He was muttering crossly as he worked. 'How can a robot possibly get laryngitis? What do you *need* it for?

Naturally enough poor K9 didn't reply. Without looking up the Doctor yelled, 'Romana!'

A girl came into the room, carrying, with some difficulty, a full-length mirror on a stand. 'Yes, Doctor?'

The Doctor looked up and blinked in astonishment. The girl who had answered his call wasn't the girl he expected. Or at least she didn't look like the girl he expected. 'Sorry, I thought you were Romana. Have you seen her? And anyway, what are you doing here?'

'Regenerating. Do you like it?'

'Nonsense, only Time Lords regenerate, and you're not a Time Lord. You're the Princess Astra, and we left you back on Atrios.' The Doctor remembered his manners. 'It's very nice to see you again, Princess Astra, but how did you get into the TARDIS? Did you stow away?'

'Doctor, I'm Romana, I tell you.' The girl set up the mirror in a corner and began studying her reflection thoughtfully.

The Doctor stared at her. The face and the body were Princess Astra's, even the voice, but there was something else . . . The essence, the personality was that of Romana. The Doctor realised that he was indeed looking at his Time Lady companion in the body of Princess Astra, or to be more accurate, in a body exactly like it.

The explanation was simple enough, at least to the Doctor. Time Lords had the power of bodily regeneration, the ability to change a damaged or worn out body for a new one by a unique and complex process of molecular readjustment. Although they weren't immortal, they went through a considerable number of reincarnations in the course of their amazingly long lives.

What surprised the Doctor was not the mere fact of Romana's regeneration, but the seeming casualness with which she was treating the occasion – not to mention the degree of regeneration control she seemed able to exercise. The Doctor's own regenerations had been rather haphazard affairs, usually in response to some kind of crisis, and the bodies he'd acquired had been very much a matter of pot luck.

Romana, on the other hand, seemed to be changing bodies as casually as she might have changed her dress. Except that the body she'd finished up with was a direct copy of someone else's. The Doctor frowned, remembering that in a purely academic sense, Romana's qualifications from the Time Lord Academy were rather higher than his own. No doubt that accounted for her superior control.

Rather reprovingly he said, 'You can't wear that body!'

'Why not? I thought it looked very nice on the Princess.'

'You can't go around wearing *copies*!'

'Well, I don't see why not.' Romana gave a twirl in front of the mirror, studying the effect of the new body and the new dress she'd chosen to go with it. 'I mean, it would be a bit embarrassing if she and I both turned up at the same party wearing identical bodies, but as we're not going back to Atrios again . . .'

The Doctor shook his head. 'No!' he said firmly. 'It just won't do. Go and try another one, go on.'

Romana sniffed indignantly, and marched out.

The Doctor went on working. Some time later a very small girl came in, and posed in front of the mirror. 'I quite like this one, but it's a bit short.'

The Doctor spoke without looking up. 'Well, go away and lengthen it.'

The small girl went out. For a time the Doctor was able to get on with his work in peace.

The peace ended when someone else strode heavily into the room.

The Doctor addressed the silent K9. 'Fancy

trying to look like someone else. It's all vanity anyway. People attach too much importance to outside appearances, it's what's inside that counts.' He looked up to see an enormously tall girl looming over him. 'No, no, no, far too big,' he said crossly. The re-transformed Romana went out again.

The Doctor worked on. Soon Romana reappeared in the guise of an exotic female of some alien race. 'Ughh! Take it away,' said the Doctor. The apparition retreated hastily.

The Doctor sighed. 'Look,' he called. 'All you want is something warm and sensible, something that will wear well, with a little style and flair to it . . .'

There was no answer from the adjoining room. Soon afterwards yet another girl appeared. She wore a long coat, high boots, a very long multi-coloured scarf, and a big floppy hat which almost covered her face. 'Like this, Doctor?'

The Doctor looked up and beamed approvingly at the outfit, which had something strangely familiar about it. 'Now that's more like it. Good heavens, that's absolutely right for you. I never knew you had such a sense of style.'

He stood up, and the girl spun round before him. 'I thought you said external appearances weren't important, Doctor.'

'Well, no, but it's nice to get them right though, isn't it? I mean, how can you go wrong with a look like this!'

The Doctor lifted the brim of the floppy hat, looked underneath and saw an attractive but very familiar face.

Romana had come almost full circle: she was back in her Princess Astra body.

'Oh, no!' groaned the Doctor.

'What's the matter, don't you like it? I think it will do very nicely. Imposing forehead, nice hair, neat little chin. The arms are a bit long, but I can always take them in a bit.'

'No, the arms are fine,' said the Doctor helplessly. 'It's just that . . .' He sighed, realising he'd been outmanoeuvred. 'Oh, all right, have it your own way.'

'Oh, good! I'll go and get rid of these silly clothes then.'

'But I *like* that outfit.'

'Never mind,' said Romana demurely. 'Remember, Doctor, it's what's inside that counts!' She turned to leave. 'Incidentally, where are we going?'

'I don't know. That's up to the randomiser, remember?'

At the end of their last adventure, Romana and the Doctor had almost been tricked into handing over the all-important Key of Time to the evil Black Guardian. At the last moment, the Doctor had tricked his adversary, scattering fragments of the Key to the far corners of the cosmos. To escape the enraged Black Guardian's revenge the Doctor had built a device called the randomiser into the directional circuits of the TARDIS. The Black Guardian could hardly discover where he was going next if he didn't know himself.

Romana shivered, feeling that they had exchanged the frying pan of the Black Guardian's revenge for the fire of any number of unknown dangers. She smiled bravely.

'Well, wherever it is, call me when we get there!'

She went away, and the Doctor continued to work on K9.

The landscape was bleak and harsh, an arid stone plain scattered with strangely angular rocks. Thunder growled menacingly in a dark and alien sky, and the very ground seemed to shiver and vibrate.

Beneath a mountain of loose rocks was an overhanging cliff edge. A wheezing, groaning sound mingled with the noise of the thunder, and the square blue shape of the TARDIS materialised directly beneath the overhang.

The thunder rumbled, the ground shook, and a scattering of loose stones began rolling down the mountainside and pattering on the roof of the TARDIS.

The Doctor was studying his instruments. 'We've arrived, Romana!' he called.

Romana's voice floated from the next room. 'What's the place like?'

'Breathable atmosphere, but a high degree of seismic activity.'

'What do you mean, psychic activity! Ghosts?'

'Lots of earthquakes.'

'Oh, *seismic*. I thought you said psychic.'

The Doctor was only half-listening. 'Side-kick?' he mumbled, baffled.

Romana misheard him. 'Like it? How do I know? I haven't seen it yet.'

The conversation didn't seem to be getting very far. 'Romana, if you want to talk to me, will you please come in here and do it properly.'

Romana came into the control room, still in her Princess Astra body, but now wearing her new outfit, tailored to fit. 'There, what do you think?'

'Very nice,' said the Doctor perfunctorily, and handed her two pills. 'Take these, will you?'

'What are they?'

'Anti-radiation capsules. The levels out there are very high.' He handed her a tiny device rather like an egg-timer. 'Here's a bleeper, it'll go off when you need the next dose.'

Romana swallowed two pills, then stowed the bleeper away in a belt-pouch, pleased that the Doctor seemed to be taking sensible precautions for once. 'Let's see where we are.' She switched on the scanner. It showed a bare rock wall.

'Oh, *very* promising,' said the Doctor.

'Well, we'd better go and take a look.'

'I suppose so.' The Doctor picked up K9's brain section and inserted it back in the case. Immediately the little automaton began rushing backwards, making rasping, whirring sounds. The Doctor dived on K9, made a quick readjustment, and the robot dog was still.

Romana looked down at him. 'What went wrong?'

'I'm afraid I forgot the most important thing my cybernetics teacher taught me.'

'What was that?'

'When replacing a robot brain, always make sure arrow "A" is pointing to the front.'

The Doctor got to his feet and opened the TARDIS's doors.

They stood outside the TARDIS looking around them. There was little to see, just an endless bare plain with a scattering of rocks, stretching away into fast-gathering darkness.

'Not the most inviting of planets, is it, Doctor?'

'You know,' said the Doctor softly, 'I have the most extraordinary feeling I've been here before!'

The sensation of familiarity, known as *déjà vu*, was a common phenomenon among time travellers.

'Just an impression, or something you actually recognise?'

'Nothing tangible. I just seem to sense something, a pervading air of . . .'

'Evil?'

'Yes . . . *evil*. You feel it too, then?'

'Shall we go back to the TARDIS and try somewhere else?'

The Doctor considered for a moment. Perhaps it would be better to go back. But his sense of curiosity was too strong for him, that and a strange feeling of – destiny. Randomiser or no, somehow the Doctor felt he had come to this planet because he was *meant* to come here. He gave Romana a look of mock-indignation. 'Go back? And leave me wondering for the rest of time where I'd been? I'd never sleep at nights!'

Determinedly the Doctor set off and, a little reluctantly, Romana followed him.

As they moved away, a few more loose rocks slithered down the mountain and rattled against the roof of the TARDIS.

They walked for some time across the featureless plain, and soon the TARDIS was swallowed up by the darkness that gathered around them. All the time great threatening claps of thunder rolled around the darkening alien sky and the ground beneath their feet seemed to shudder in response.

The Doctor stopped and picked up a handful of

pebbles, studying them thoughtfully. 'Interesting.'

'Precious stones?'

'Only in the archaeological sense – but in that way, they could be more valuable than diamonds.' He looked round. 'I need a larger sample to be certain. Ah, there we are!'

The Doctor pointed to a squarish rock, half buried in the ground. He knelt beside it and cleared away the surrounding rubble, rubbing the lichen from the rock's smooth surface. 'Yes, I was right – as usual!'

'How modest, Doctor.'

'See what you can make of it,' challenged the Doctor.

Romana knelt and studied the block. 'Some kind of composite material . . . gravel in a binding of limestone and clay.'

The Doctor nodded approvingly. 'And limestone and clay make . . . ?'

'Cement.'

'Correct! And if you add gravel you get . . .?'

'Concrete?'

'Congratulations, Romana, you have all the makings of a first-class navvy! Yes, concrete, or the closest alternative this planet can produce. The point is, it was manufactured, Romana. Manufactured.' The Doctor gestured at the endless rocky plain around them. 'All this rock and stone, all these fragments, all manufactured. Brick, concrete, plaster, cement, all pounded and pulverised, reduced to rubble.' He straightened up. 'We're walking across the remains of what was once a great city. A great city, brought to dust. But by what?'

The only answer was another roll of thunder.

15

2

Underground Evil

'What about the people who lived here?' said Romana. 'What happened to them?' She looked at the grey desolation all around them and then back at the Doctor. 'Those tremors we felt . . . maybe they destroyed the city?'

The Doctor wasn't listening. He stood, head cocked, trying to pick up some distant sound. Above the eerie moaning of the wind came a faint, whining, whirring sound, as if some kind of powerful machinery was in operation some distance away.

'You hear it?'

Romana pointed. 'It seems to be coming from over there.'

'Then that's the direction we'll take!'

Some time later, after an interminable journey across the grey stone plain, they were standing amidst a pile of enormous concrete blocks which were strewn haphazardly across the plain, as though some giant child had knocked over a pile of building blocks. It was obvious that they were the scattered and broken remains of some colossal building.

Romana said, 'Buildings this size don't just fall down. Maybe it was earthquakes after all.'

'It was something pretty devastating. But remember the radioactivity – '

The Doctor broke off as the ground began to quake and shudder beneath their feet. The whining of machinery had started up again. Romana said nervously, 'Well, whatever it is, it looks as if it's happening again!'

'It's pretty close now,' shouted the Doctor, and indeed it was. The sound seemed to be coming from directly under their feet. Soon it wasn't just a whine but a great howling scream, accompanied by a shuddering vibration that seemed to jar every nerve in their bodies. Loose rocks rattled and bounced on the stony ground, the concrete blocks groaned and creaked, and the Doctor and Romana clutched each other for support. The screaming rose to an unbearable crescendo, then suddenly, mercifully it cut off, leaving a silence that almost seemed to hurt.

The Doctor shook his head and stuck his finger in his ears. 'Anything broken?'

'Only my nerve! I feel as if every bone in my body has been disconnected. That was drilling equipment, wasn't it?'

'Maybe we've struck an underground dentist! Let's get going before it starts up again.'

They moved on past the scattered concrete blocks. Behind them the whirring of the great underground drill had started up again, and they moved faster, hurrying away from the shaking ground and the unbearable, bone-jarring howl.

Eventually the sound died away behind them. The Doctor led the way round yet another huge concrete block. Suddenly he ducked back into cover, motioning Romana not to move.

He peered round the edge of the block, and Romana crept up to join him.

Before them was a strange and eerie sight.

Directly ahead was an open space, a kind of amphitheatre, ringed by jagged blocks. Across this space, a weird-looking group was moving slowly and silently towards them. There were six of them, and they were human, or at least humanoid in form. They wore the tattered and grimy remnants of what might once have been some kind of uniform. Strangest of all, their hair and skin were a dead, unearthly white.

Leading the little procession was a woman, a smokily blazing torch held above her head.

Behind her came four men, carrying a kind of crude stretcher, raised shoulder high. A body lay on the stretcher.

Behind them came the sixth and last member of the party, another woman. She too was carrying a blazing torch.

It was quite obvious what was happening. The scene could have been duplicated on innumerable planets, in countless societies. The man on the stretcher was dead, and this was his funeral procession.

In the centre of the open area the procession halted. The stretcher was lowered reverently to the ground. The women with the torches stood motionless at the head and feet of the corpse, while the four men began gathering loose pieces of rubble and building a kind of long, low cairn over the body. They worked with swift urgency, and soon the body was completely hidden by rocks.

When the work was done, one of the women found a flat piece of stone, scratched a few symbols on it with a piece of pointed rock, and propped it against the head of the cairn.

For a while the two women and the four men stood grouped around the funeral mound, heads bowed in silent communion, mourning their dead. Then they turned and moved away into the darkness.

'Why do they leave their dead on the surface, covered with stones?' whispered Romana. 'Why don't they bury them?'

'Adaptation to local conditions. Just you try digging a six-foot hole through concrete rubble!'

'They were so silent, Doctor. So slow, they moved like the living dead!'

'The living dead,' repeated the Doctor softly. 'Zombies! Perhaps we've found a planet where zombies rule.'

'Shut up!'

'Coming with me?'

'Where?'

'We want to know more about this planet, don't we? This is a chance to find out.'

'How?'

'By examining that body.'

'Doctor, you can't . . .'

'Why not? Apart from one basic difference, the dead are very much like the living.'

'Your reasoning is very logical, Doctor – but I think I'll stay here and keep watch, if you don't mind!'

'I'd appreciate that.' The Doctor began creeping away, and then paused. 'By the way, if you should meet one of *them* . . . you can always tell a genuine zombie by its skin. It feels icy cold to the touch!'

The Doctor slipped away. Romana shivered, as if she could already feel an icy hand upon her shoulder. It was a legend common to many planets and many cultures, she thought: the walking dead, brought back from the grave, usually to act as slaves for some evil sorcerer. But of course it was only a legend – wasn't it?

The Doctor headed towards the burial mound, smiling a little guiltily to himself. Perhaps it had been unfair to make Romana's flesh creep like that, but her icy Time Lady composure sometimes got on his nerves. He hadn't been able to resist the chance of shaking it just a little.

He reached the mound and began pulling away the stones, all thought of supernatural terrors driven out by scientific curiosity. Very soon he had uncovered the dead man's face. It was thin and wasted, hair and skin ghastly white. He cleared more stones and uncovered the upper part of the body. As he had suspected, the uniform proved to be an astronaut-type coverall, its breast marked with military insignia. Gently, the Doctor unsealed a pocket and took out a plastic wallet. He examined the contents for a moment, and nodded thoughtfully to himself. He pocketed the wallet and began working his way back towards Romana.

Romana, meanwhile, was sitting huddled against her rock, trying to convince herself that the faint night sounds all around her were completely natural, nothing at all to worry about.

She glanced back at the burial mound and saw the Doctor had gone. She guessed he was moving back towards her, temporarily out of sight behind one of the chunks of masonry, but his sudden disappearance was somehow unnerving all the same.

She turned round in a slow circle, peering into the surrounding darkness. Was that the sound of stealthy movement she could hear? 'Doctor?' she called nervously. 'Doctor, is that you out there?'

A white hand reached out and touched her on the shoulder . . .

She spun round with a gasp of terror – and saw the Doctor, who had just appeared round the side of the giant block.

'I wish you wouldn't do that,' she said angrily.

'Sorry, did I startle you?'

'Oh no, of course not! Doctor, look at your hands!'

The Doctor looked. His hands were a ghastly white. He brushed them against his coat, leaving a trail of fine white dust.

'Well, did you discover anything?'

He produced the plastic wallet. 'The deceased was Space Major Dal Garrant, a combat pilot serving with the Third Galactic Fleet. Home planet, Kantra.'

'Kantra? That's a tropical planet, nothing like this place at all.'

'That's right. A trifle humid for my taste, but quite attractive in its way.'

'What's a Kantrian doing living, or rather dying, here?'

'Odd, isn't it? He died of a combination of malnutrition and exhaustion, by the way.'

'Hardly surprising in a place like this.'

'Except that he ought to have died of radiation poisoning first,' said the Doctor slowly. He held up his box of capsules. 'The Kantrians haven't developed bio-technology to this level yet, so . . .'

Suddenly, there was a screaming roaring sound, from above not below this time. A fierce blue light streaked rapidly through the night sky overhead.

'A space ship!' said Romana.

'That's right. And it's landing on the other side of that rise. Come on!'

They reached the top of the rise just in time to see the space ship coming down to land. It was saucer-shaped, revolving rapidly, so that details were obscured in a blur of spinning lights.

'Recognise the type, Romana?'

'Hard to tell under these conditions. Judging by the size and general design, a space cruiser of inter-galactic range with time warp capacity. Possible origin Star System 4X Alpha 4.'

'Well, I haven't got my *Janes Book of Space Craft* with me,' said the Doctor gravely, 'but by and large, I think I agree.'

The space ship touched the planetary surface sending up an immense cloud of fine white dust. When the dust cleared they saw to their surprise that the ship was still spinning – sinking deeper and deeper into the ground. When the motion finally stopped, only a small pointed turret was left above ground, projecting from the surface like the conning tower of a submarine. 'Interesting technique,' said the Doctor thoughtfully. 'Camouflage and protection rolled into one!'

Romana looked at the inconspicuous mound, all that remained visible of the huge, gleaming space ship. 'Well, for a place that looked dead to start with, there's certainly a lot going on here.'

The Doctor grinned. 'We've probably arrived at the beginning of the tourist season. How far away would you say that ship is?'

'Not more than a mile.'

'Just the right distance for a nice bracing walk!'

'You want to go down there?'

'It would be ungracious not to go and welcome our visitors. We can always say we're from the Tourist Board!'

They began to descend the slope.

If it was only a mile to the space ship, it was a very long one, thought Romana. They plodded across the plain and somehow the ship didn't seem to be getting any nearer.

Romana's attention was drawn to a group of massive shapes just off to their left. At first she had thought they were more of the enormous blocks, but as they came closer she saw that these were actual buildings, ruined and roofless, but with the original shapes still clearly discernible. For some reason the devastation which had overtaken the planet seemed slightly less complete just here. She was about to suggest to the Doctor that they go and explore them, when there was the sudden *crump* of an explosion.

'That sounded awfully close,' said Romana uneasily. 'What do you think it was?'

'Sounded like some kind of land mine, or a bomb.'

There was another explosion, and then another. They were getting closer.

'Look!' screamed Romana. A line of explosions was moving rapidly across the plain towards them, one after another, as though someone was setting off a whole series of bombs.

'We'd better get under cover,' yelled the Doctor.

'This way!' shouted Romana, and began running towards the group of ruined buildings.

The Doctor followed, but the explosions seemed to be chasing after them.

They dashed inside a vast, partly roofless pillared hall, and crouched down behind a ruined wall.

The line of explosions came closer, closer . . .

The hall began to shudder and vibrate. Several pillars actually collapsed and a chunk of wall fell, far too close to them for comfort. The explosions came closer, closer still – and then passed by, disappearing in the distance.

Romana gave a sigh of relief. 'What was all that, Doctor? Were they firing at us from the ship?'

'I don't think so. The explosions are just a by-product. Someone's blasting away the rubble down there, using high-impact phason drills.'

'On a ruined planet like this?'

'Apparently. And since it can hardly be the natives, that someone must be importing some pretty powerful technology.'

One of the room's supporting pillars, broken almost in two by the explosions, chose this precise moment to give way. It cracked, wavered and began toppling slowly, almost majestically towards them, bringing a section of roof down with it.

'Look out!' screamed Romana. But she was too late.

The pillar collapsed, burying them under a pile of rubble.

3

The Daleks

Romana struggled desperately to free herself. To her astonishment she found she could manage it fairly easily. She was bruised and shaken, but she didn't seem to be much hurt.

The Doctor had been considerably less fortunate. The lower part of the toppling pillar had fallen across his body, pinning him to the ground. He lay still as death, his eyes closed.

Romana struggled across to him. 'Doctor, can you hear me?'

The Doctor didn't move or speak.

Romana tried to shift the column, but it was far too heavy. She grabbed his shoulders, trying to pull him clear. As she heaved and tugged away, the Doctor opened his eyes and said peevishly, 'Can't a fellow get any sleep around here?'

'Doctor, are you all right?'

'Hard to tell. I can't see most of me.' He waggled his toes. 'My extremities seem unimpaired. No pain, but I'm being squashed. Can you take any of the weight of the column? Maybe I could wriggle out.'

Romana tried once more to shift the column, but she couldn't move it an inch. She examined the pile of stones around the Doctor. 'I think you're not so much squashed, as wedged into a gap. The main weight seems to be on this chunk of concrete here. Lucky for you, or you'd have been flattened. I'm afraid to interfere too much in case the block shifts and the whole pile comes down on top of you.'

The Doctor considered. 'It looks as if we're not going to move it without help. I daresay K9 could blast me free. Do you think you could go and get him?' The Doctor managed a smile. 'I'd go myself, but I'm detained by some rather pressing business.'

'Yes, of course. I'll be as quick as I can. Will you be all right?'

'Who can tell?' said the Doctor ruefully. 'Who can tell? I'd appreciate it if you'd hurry, though.'

'I'll be as quick as I can. Don't go away, will you?'

The Doctor winced. 'I rather hoped you'd resist the temptation to say that! And remember, arrow "A" to the front!'

'Shan't be long.' Romana hurried off and the Doctor settled himself to wait.

Since the upper part of his body was free and he wasn't in actual pain, he was able to make himself reasonably comfortable. He found a suitable piece of granite to use as a pillow, fished a copy of *The Origins of the Tenth Galaxy* from his pocket and settled back to read. After a page or two, he put down the book with a scornful laugh. 'The man's a fool. "Origins of the Tenth Galaxy" indeed! Why doesn't he ask someone who was there!'

Romana retraced the journey she'd taken with the Doctor, back across the plain with its huge scattered concrete blocks, past the open space where they'd seen the corpse being buried – the burial mound made a useful landmark.

The journey had been spooky enough with the

Doctor, but it was doubly so now that she was on her own. She heard the distant high-pitched whine of underground drilling, and the distant rumble of more explosions. The night wind howled eerily. Romana began to get the strangest impression that she was being followed. Once she spun round and thought she saw a furtive figure duck back into cover. She waited for a moment but the sinister shape didn't reappear, and Romana turned and ran on.

Soon she was dashing straight ahead in blind panic, slipping and stumbling, scrambling to her feet to continue her flight. She staggered on until she collapsed in near exhaustion. For a moment she just lay there, too tired to move. Wearily she got to her feet – and saw the TARDIS nestling under its overhang just a short distance in front of her.

Joyfully she began running towards it – only to be blasted from her feet as a sudden sequence of explosions erupted across the area between the TARDIS and where she stood. She hugged the ground and a shower of debris rained down on her.

At last the explosions stopped and cautiously she lifted her head. To her relief, the ground between her and the TARDIS, although churned up by the explosions, was easy enough to cross. But when she reached the TARDIS, another shock was awaiting her: the explosions had dislodged the overhang, and the police box was half buried in rubble.

The door was completely blocked.

Romana scrambled over the rock-pile and hammered on the upper part of the TARDIS. 'K9!' she called. 'K9, can you hear me?'

There was no reply.

Romana tried to clear away the stones, but the

chunks of masonry were far too big to lift.

She scrambled down from the pile and stood wondering what to do next. Suddenly there was a sharp buzz from inside her belt-pouch – the bleeper the Doctor had given her. It was time to take another anti-radiation pill. Romana began searching through the pouch – and remembered that although she had the bleeper, the Doctor had the pills. Wearily she turned, and began retracing her steps. She was too tired and depressed to notice the tall, gaunt figure that was stalking her determinedly across the plain.

The Doctor took his radiation pills, and put the bottle back in his pocket. He reminded himself that it was also time for Romana to take hers – still, she should be back with K9 soon, and a brief delay wouldn't do her any real harm.

Sheer boredom drove the Doctor back to his book. It had been written by a particularly pompous Time Lord historian, someone the Doctor had never cared for, and he was getting a certain pleasure from picking out the book's many errors. He began reading aloud to cheer himself up. '"The conditions on the planet Magla make it incapable of supporting any kind of life-form." Ha! The old fool obviously doesn't realise that Magla *is* a life form, an eight-thousand-mile-wide amoeba that's grown itself a crusty shell!'

The Doctor was turning the pages in search of new errors, when he heard footsteps. 'Welcome back, Romana. What kept you?'

There was no reply.

The Doctor looked up and saw two strangers. One male, one female, both tall, well-built, and exceptionally handsome. Both wore simple, military-type space coveralls. Both carried hand-blasters, which were pointing straight at the Doctor.

The Doctor raised his hat. 'Good evening to you! Forgive me if I don't rise.'

The two strangers didn't smile. Menacingly, they advanced towards him . . .

Some time later, Romana ran into the ruined chamber. 'Doctor, I couldn't get – '

She broke off, in utter astonishment. The pillar that had pinned the Doctor to the ground was still there, the Doctor's discarded book lay just beside it.

The Doctor was gone.

Perhaps he had managed to free himself after all, thought Romana. Trust him, after sending her all that way. Now he'd wandered off somewhere. Typical!

'Doctor,' she called. 'Doctor, where are you?'

There was no reply.

She heard footsteps approaching the doorway. Her first thought was that it must be the Doctor coming back and she moved to the doorway to meet him.

Then she hesitated. Those footsteps didn't sound like the Doctor – they were furtive, stealthy. And if it was the Doctor, why hadn't he answered her call?

She flattened herself against the broken wall, and waited.

A tall gaunt figure appeared in the doorway. It had white hair and white skin, like the members of the burial party they'd seen earlier. Its sunken eyes seemed to burn as they swept round the room.

Romana backed away, moving further and further into the darkness. Suddenly the ground vanished beneath her feet, and with a scream she vanished into black nothingness.

The watcher moved slowly forward and stared down the shaft into which Romana had fallen.

Romana was sliding helplessly down the shaft. It was lined with polished stone, and she was quite unable to stop herself moving.

At last she shot out of the shaft, fell a few more feet, and landed with a bone-jarring thud on a hard stone floor.

For a moment she was too shocked to move. Slowly, she struggled to her feet. She was shaken and bruised, but to her relief nothing seemed to be broken.

She was in a stone-walled underground chamber, with no way in or out apart from the shaft down which she had fallen. She could see the opening of the shaft just above her head and leaped up, trying to get a grip on the edge. But her fingers slipped on the polished stone and she fell to the ground.

In the hall above, the watcher was unwinding a coil of rope from around his waist. He fastened one end around the base of a pillar, and began paying out the rest, moving towards the pit . . .

Romana made several more attempts to get back into the shaft, but each time her fingers slipped and she fell back. Too tired to try again, she stood looking around her prison. There was little enough to see, just four stone walls and the opening of the shaft, tantalisingly out of reach.

The cell began to vibrate. She could feel the walls shuddering, and hear a high-pitched whine of machinery moving ever closer.

Cracks began to appear in the wall directly opposite. The cracks formed a kind of arch-shape, and suddenly the entire centre of the wall seemed to crumble inwards, leaving a great black hole.

With terrifying speed, two metallic shapes glided through the arch. They were shaped like huge metal-studded pepper pots, they had projecting metal arms and an eye-lens on a kind of metal stalk. They swept menacingly down on Romana, crowding her back against the wall, hemming her in so that there was no escape. In harsh metallic voices they screeched, 'Do not move! Do not move or you will be exterminated! You are a prisoner of the Daleks!'

4

The Movellans

Frozen with terror, Romana obeyed the grating metallic commands. One of the Daleks ordered, 'Scan the prisoner for concealed weapons.'

The second Dalek glided forward and swept a metal arm across Romana's body. There was a faint buzzing sound. 'The prisoner is unarmed.'

The first Dalek said, 'At my command you will move forward. Any attempt to escape will be severely punished. No further warning will be given. Is that understood?'

Romana nodded dumbly.

'Is that understood?' screeched the Dalek angrily. 'Speak! Speak! Speak!'

'Yes,' shouted Romana. 'Yes, I understand!'

'The prisoner will be taken to interrogation. Follow!'

One Dalek glided through the black hole in the wall. The other held back, waiting for Romana. Obediently she went through the hole and the Dalek glided after her.

Hanging from his rope inside the shaft, the gaunt stranger watched them go. When they were clear of the chamber, he began climbing back up the shaft.

The girl stranger had been taken by the Daleks. There was nothing he could do for her now. There was nothing anyone could do.

The control room of the buried space ship was huge, brightly lit, impressive in its functional simplicity. Looking around him, the Doctor realised that the simple elegance of design was the product of a very high degree of technology indeed.

Men and women were moving about the flight deck. They wore immaculate space uniforms, they were tall, well-built and extraordinarily good-looking. Whoever his rescuers were, thought the Doctor, they were a strikingly attractive people.

His mind went back briefly over recent events. Once the two strangers had registered that the pinioned, helpless Doctor was hardly a danger to them, they had holstered their blasters and moved forward. In an astonishing display of strength and co-ordination, they had seized hold of the pillar between them, and lifted it sufficiently for him to scramble free.

Ignoring both his thanks and his questions, they had led him out of the chamber, across the stony plain, and through the entrance hatch of their buried space ship. And now here he was.

The Doctor noticed that some of the space ship crew were moving in a steady procession to a kind of computerised dispenser. From it they took slender silver tubes which they slotted into their belts. Tools, wondered the Doctor, or supplies? Radiation pills perhaps, like these he was carrying himself? Dismissing the problem, he looked up as one of the aliens came over to him. He was tall and handsome like the rest and the insignia on his uniform seemed to signify superior rank. He spoke in a deep, mellow voice. 'I am Commander Sharrel.' He indicated the Doctor's two rescuers who had followed him across the control room. 'This is Lan and this is Agella. I am glad they were able to help you.'

'Charming people, both of them,' said the Doctor politely. 'Strong, too. They lifted that column off me as though it were a matchstick. I can't think where they hide their muscles. I'm the Doctor, by the way.'

'All Movellan crew are in peak physical condition,' said Commander Sharrel solemnly. 'It is an essential qualification.'

The Doctor looked at the busy scene around him. A number of the Movellans were seated at video-consoles. They wore headphones and seemed to be studying patterns of flickering lights running across their screens. 'And what are they doing now? A scanning exercise, perhaps?'

Commander Sharrel smiled politely, but he did not reply.

Undaunted, the Doctor went on, 'I hate to seem inquisitive, but I could do with a little information. What brings you to . . . ? By the way, what is the name of this planet?'

'You do not know where you are?'

'Well, not exactly. I had a little problem with my directional equipment.'

'I see. You made a forced landing?'

'Something of the sort.'

'I understand. This planet is listed in our Movellan star charts as D Five Gamma Z Alpha.'

'I'm afraid that's not much help to me. I'm old-fashioned, I prefer to stick to names. What brings *you* here?'

'I am sorry, Doctor. The nature of our mission must remain secret. I am sure you will understand.'

'Oh, certainly, certainly. I just thought an exchange

of information might be mutually helpful.'

'Perhaps. Have you learned anything, since you landed?'

'Not much,' admitted the Doctor. 'I saw a man being buried though. He was from Kantria.'

Commander Sharrel was giving nothing away. 'And are you of the opinion that this planet is Kantria?'

'No, I know Kantria. Besides, there were a few words scratched on his headstone . . . I understand enough Kantrian to translate them. They read "Far from his native world".'

'What else have you observed?'

'A considerable number of surface explosions. I think they must be recoil action, from phason drills, being used deep underground.' The Doctor spread his hands. 'That's all, I'm afraid.'

Commander Sharrel paused, exchanging glances with Lan and Agella. 'I think there is at least one thing I can tell you without breaking security. Our mission here is directed against a species known as the Daleks . . .'

'The Daleks?' The Doctor jumped up in alarm.

'They are a race of evil automatons – '

'You don't have to tell me about the Daleks. I know a great deal about them already.'

Now it was Commander Sharrel's turn to be astonished. 'You know the Daleks?'

'Oh, yes,' said the Doctor. 'I know the Daleks. Better than you can possibly imagine!'

Deep beneath the surface of the ruined planet, the Daleks had set up their base. Fresh air and daylight meant nothing to them, and an underground setting was their natural habitat.

Romana was taken into a brightly-lit underground area with complex pieces of scientific equipment dotted about the floor. The architecture of the base was harsh and bleakly metallic, and it had the improvised air of the headquarters of some kind of field expedition. Romana saw that the metal walls held illuminated blow-ups of charts or maps, rather like architectural drawings. Daleks bustled to and fro, scanning them, returning to instrument consoles to study their readings.

Romana was taken to a sinister-looking machine, and directed to stand against it. It was a skeletal metal framework, connected to a console. There were arm-rests at shoulder height, and at the end of the arm-rests were two glowing metal orbs.

'You will grasp the orbs,' ordered a Dalek. Apprehensively, Romana did as she was told. She felt no pain, but a slight, electric tingle spread through her body.

The Dalek began bombarding her with questions. Who was she? Why had she come to the planet? Where were her companions? What were they doing now? There were many other questions, most of which she couldn't even understand, let alone reply to.

'Answer!' grated the Dalek. 'Answer! Answer! Answer!'

'I don't know the answers,' shouted Romana angrily. 'I don't even understand the questions. Why don't you leave me alone?'

Her outburst produced an astonished silence. The Dalek at the controls of the interrogation machine studied the pattern of flashing lights and symbols on its read-out screen. 'Detector indicates truthful response.'

The Dalek in charge of the interrogation said, 'We will continue.'

Wearily Romana rubbed her hand over her eyes. The Dalek's sucker-arm seized her wrist, forcing it back onto the globe. 'You will not remove your hands from the sensor globes.'

The Dalek paused as if considering its approach. 'Statement. Your purpose here was to sabotage Dalek operations. True or false?'

'I didn't even know there were any Dalek operations here,' began Romana.

'Answer,' shrieked the Dalek. 'Answer true or false. Answer! Answer! Answer!'

'False!' yelled Romana.

'Detector indicates truthful response.'

'Statement. You are in the employ of hostile space power and have been sent here to spy on the Daleks. True or false?'

'False, false, false!' shouted Romana. 'Now shut up and leave me alone.'

'Detector indicates truthful response. Standard basic interrogation now complete.' There were whirrs and clicks and flashing lights from the console.

'Report analysis of responses.'

'Analysis indicates subject in category nine.'

'Category nine subjects represent no threat to Dalek security. The prisoner will leave interrogation machine.'

Thankfully, Romana let go of the glowing globes. 'Does that mean I can go?'

'As a humanoid, you are a useful low-grade work

unit. You have no other value. You will be given anti-radiation treatment, and assigned to the labour force.'

'What are you talking about? I'm not going to be in any labour force.'

'You will obey all Dalek commands instantly. You will complete your daily work schedule. Do this, and you will be allowed to live. Fail, and you will be exterminated.'

The Daleks gathered round Romana in a menacing circle.

'Obey all Dalek commands.'

'Obey instantly.'

'Obey without question!'

The harsh metallic voices rose in terrifying chorus. 'Obey! Obey! Obey! Obey! Obey!'

Romana clapped her hands over her ears, but the grating voices could not be shut out.

'Obey the Daleks! Obey! Obey! Obey!'

'Commander Sharrel, please, you *must* believe me. It's vital that you tell me what you know about the Dalek mission on this planet. I've had considerable experience of their methods. I'm sure I can help you, but first I must know why they're here.'

'Doctor, that is exactly what I need to know myself – ' Commander Sharrel broke off as Agella hurried up to him. 'Yes, what is it?'

'Excuse me, Commander, but the perimeter patrol has picked someone up. He was wandering about, close to the ship. Do you want to see him?'

'Bring him in at once.'

Two Movellans entered, bringing a strange figure between them. He was tall and gaunt with white face and white hair, and he wore the tattered remnants of some kind of space uniform. He looked dazedly around at the technological neatness of his surroundings, the brightly-lit instrument panels, the smartly uniformed Movellans with their brisk, disciplined movements. As his eyes took all this in, some long-buried memory seemed to stir deep within him.

He came to a halt in front of Commander Sharrel and straightened up in a pitiful attempt to come to attention.

Commander Sharrel said, 'Report, please. Name, rank, planet of origin and fleet attachment. What is your purpose on this planet?'

In a hoarse, weary voice, the newcomer said, 'Starship Engineer Tyssan, sir. Serving with the Deep Space Fleet out of Planet Earth. I was captured two years ago . . .' His voice faltered and began to waver. Feebly he went on, 'Since then, I have been a prisoner of the Daleks . . .'

The effort of making a proper military report had been too much for Engineer Tyssan. He staggered and toppled to the ground, falling stiffly like a cut-down tree.

The Doctor sprang forward, catching him and lowering him to the floor. He knelt to examine the unconscious man.

'What's the matter with him?' demanded Sharrel.

'Oh, nothing much! Malnutrition, exhaustion, a dose of radiation poisoning.' The Doctor looked up, his face bleak. 'Put more simply he's been half starved, kept in inhuman conditions, and worked almost to death. He was telling you the truth, Commander. He's been a prisoner of the Daleks!'

5

Slaves of the Daleks

Romana was taken to an enormous underground cavern, formed by the meeting point of a number of tunnels. It was piled high with rubble, produced by Dalek drilling operations.

Human and humanoid prisoners were piling this rubble into baskets, then tipping the baskets into huge metal skips and trundling them away. All the workers were gaunt and ragged, all had clothes, hair and skin covered with white dust. They looked like a crowd of weary ghosts. Dalek guards glided constantly to and fro.

A Dalek thrust Romana into the cavern. 'Work!' Its sucker arm indicated a pile of empty baskets. Romana picked up a basket and joined the others.

She worked in silence for a while, waiting until the Dalek guard had moved away. Then she edged towards the other prisoners. A man and a girl were working together quite close to her, and Romana moved over to join them. 'My name's Romana. What's yours?'

The girl said quietly, 'Veldan. This is Jall.'

'How long have the Daleks been holding you prisoner?'

Veldan rubbed a hand across her dust-smeared face. 'It seems like forever.'

'How did they capture you?'

'Raided our colony on Sirrian. Took about fifty of us.'

'What about you, Jall?'

'I was a passenger on a space shuttle. The Daleks attacked and scooped up the lot of us. Crew, passengers, everybody.'

'You were captured in different places, but you both ended up here?'

'They put us on a prison ship in deep space first. Hundreds of us crammed into metal cells. Life expectancy's pretty short. Then they picked about fifty of us and sent us here.' Jall laughed bitterly. 'We thought we were lucky – thought we might be able to escape. A lot of us have died since then.'

'Why can't you escape? I saw some kind of burial party earlier – it wasn't even guarded.'

It was Veldan who answered. 'For a start, there's nowhere to escape *to*. The whole planet seems to be in ruins, no food, no water, nothing. Without the radiation pills the Daleks hand out, you die in a matter of days. And every time somebody runs off, the Daleks kill some of us. Escape plans aren't very popular any more.'

Romana looked around the crowd of toiling captives. 'The Daleks brought you all here just for this? Why don't they just use machines?'

'They've got machines, huge ones to do the drilling,' said Jall. 'But for this kind of clearing up operation there's nothing as adaptable as a humanoid.'

'Cheap, expendable, easily replaced,' said Veldan bitterly. 'Whenever they die off you just go and capture some more.'

'Maybe the Daleks enjoy subjugating humanoid races,' said Romana thoughtfully. 'After all, they used to be humanoid themselves once . . .'

'How do you know so much about them?'

Before Romana could reply, a Dalek guard moved closer. 'Silence! You will remain silent at all times!'

Jall and Veldan began tossing rocks into their basket, and Romana did the same. She had been working for only a few moments when a wave of giddiness came over her, and she had to stop.

'Are you all right?' whispered Veldan.

'Still feeling a bit shaky. I got a big dose of radiation before I was captured, and I don't think it's worn off yet. I'll be all right soon. The Daleks gave me some pills . . .'

Rallying herself, Romana went on working. 'Listen you two, I've got to get away from here. Are you interested?'

'Forget it,' said Jall coldly. 'I've told you what happens if anyone tries to escape. Do you want to get innocent people killed?'

Before Romana could reply, another wave of giddiness swept over her, and she slumped forward over her basket.

Veldan and Jall moved to help her, but a Dalek guard drove them off. 'Keep away!'

'She's ill,' protested Veldan.

'Keep away.' The Dalek glided up to Romana, training its gun-stick on her body. 'Continue your work. Those unfit for work will be exterminated!'

With a mighty effort Romana struggled to her knees and began throwing chunks of rock into the metal basket. 'It's all right,' she muttered. 'I'll be all right.'

The Dalek watched her for a moment longer, and then went away.

Romana worked as slowly as she dared, eyes

moving about the cavern, checking the position of the Dalek guards. If she waited till she felt a little stronger and then made a run for one of the tunnels . . .

Veldan edged closer. 'Romana, you've got to forget about escaping. Believe me, the only way you get out of here is when you're dead.'

Romana stared at her, the girl's words echoing in her mind. 'The only way you get out of here is when you're dead . . .'

The escaped prisoner Tyssan had been given medical attention, water and food. Conscious again, though still very weak, he was talking to Commander Sharrel and the Doctor, doing his best to answer their questions.

'Do you have any idea what the Daleks are mining *for*?' asked the Doctor.

'None at all,' said Tyssan wearily. 'They don't take prisoners into their confidence.'

'How did you manage to escape?' asked Commander Sharrel.

'I was on a work party – I just collapsed. I was in a pretty bad way by then, they must have thought I was dead. When I woke up there were no Dalek guards around. They'd just left me. I managed to steal some food and water and make my way to the surface. Not that it did me much good.'

'Continue.'

Tyssan nodded towards the Doctor. 'Well, I'd been on the run for a couple of days and I spotted you and the girl.'

'Why didn't you speak to us?'

'I think I must have been a bit delirious by then. I was frightened, I didn't know who you were, what sort of reception I'd get. I followed you for a while, lost you, and then picked up the girl again. I tried to speak to her but she ran away, fell into a kind of shaft in one of the ruins.'

'Was she hurt? Why didn't you help her?'

'I tried . . . I went down the shaft after her, but I was too late, the Daleks got her.'

The Doctor jumped up. 'What? Are you sure of that?'

'Certain. I saw them take her away.'

Immediately, the Doctor started making plans. 'Presumably they'll want to interrogate her, find out where she came from. Tyssan, I've got to get into the Dalek base. Can you show me a way in?'

'I think so,' said Tyssan hesitantly. 'But you'd be taking a tremendous risk.'

'I'm used to that! Can you do it, Tyssan? Will you help me?'

The Doctor's energy and enthusiasm were infectious, and Tyssan said, 'All right, I'll try.'

'Splendid! Come on, we must get started right away!'

As the Doctor headed for the door, Commander Sharrel snapped, 'Just a minute, Doctor.'

The Doctor turned.

Commander Sharrel said, 'You may need some help. We'll go with you. Agella, go and draw some weapons.'

Moving with the calm deliberation of all the Movellans, Agella headed for the door, pausing by the computer-rack to take one of the little silver tubes and slot it into her belt.

44

'Please, hurry,' said the Doctor impatiently.

Ignoring him, Agella went calmly on her way.

In the cavern everything was quiet. Cowed and weary prisoners worked silently on their endless tasks. The Dalek guards glided menacingly to and fro.

Suddenly Romana staggered to her feet, took a few stumbling paces forward, and then pitched headlong to the ground.

Veldan went to help her, but a Dalek guard chased her away. 'Leave the prisoner. Return to your work.'

'But she's ill . . .'

'Return to your work!'

Reluctantly Veldan obeyed. The Dalek glided closer to Romana and moved its 'sucker', in reality a sensitive scanning device, across her body. 'There is no respiration, no heartbeat. This prisoner is dead.'

The Dalek turned away.

'You can't just leave her there,' shouted Jall. 'At least let us bury her.'

The Dalek swung round, menacing him with its gun. 'The prisoner is dead. You will be permitted to dispose of her when the work cycle is complete. Return to your work. You will obey!'

Jall obeyed.

Tyssan climbed cautiously down the rope into the shaft. The chamber was empty now. In the far wall was the gaping hole drilled by the Daleks.

Tyssan dropped down into the chamber and called up the shaft. 'It's all clear. Come on!'

The Doctor slid down the rope, followed by Agella, Lan and Commander Sharrel.

Tyssan pointed. 'The Daleks came through there, so there must be a way through to their workings.' He shivered at the thought of the hell from which he had so recently escaped.

The Doctor noticed his reaction. 'You've done enough by showing us the way in, Tyssan. Believe me, I'm more than grateful. There's no need for you to take any more chances. Why don't you go back to the Movellan ship? They'll look after you.'

Tyssan looked tempted, but he shook his head. 'I'll stay, I've got nothing to lose. Ever since they brought me here, I've had a premonition I was going to die on Skaro.'

'Skaro? Are you telling me this is *Skaro*? The planet where the Daleks first originated?'

'Of course, Doctor. Didn't you know?'

The Doctor looked at Commander Sharrel. 'Is he right?'

'We believe so, Doctor.'

The Doctor shook his head wonderingly. 'So, the Daleks have returned to Skaro, to the place of their creation. I should have known . . .'

'If your navigation instruments weren't working, you couldn't know.'

'I'm not talking about instruments. The aura of evil, the feeling that I'd been here before . . . I should have trusted my instincts.'

The Doctor rose and stared into the darkness beyond the hole. 'Why? Why are they burrowing in the ruins of their city. For what?'

He broke off, his eyes widening. 'No,' he whispered. 'No, it couldn't be. It would be too fantastic, even for the Daleks . . .'

'What would?' demanded Commander Sharrel.

The Doctor shrugged. 'Just a wild theory. There's probably nothing in it. Anyway, we'll find the answers we want in Dalek control.' He led them through the archway.

In the Dalek control area, Dalek technicians were moving about instrument consoles, working with quiet efficiency. A Dalek engineer glided in through an archway, and came up to the Dalek leader.

'Vertical drill three is in position.'

'Penetration to lower levels will commence immediately. Order that drilling is to continue until penetration is complete.'

'I obey.'

There was a sudden bleeping from a nearby control panel, and the Dalek leader turned to the technician at the controls. 'Report!'

'Security sensors detect unauthorised movement in sector seven.'

'Despatch units four and six to investigate.'

'I obey!'

The technician moved to a communications circuit, and sent a rapid signal.

From the nearby security section, two Daleks set off in search of the intruders.

6

Escape

The Doctor and his party moved cautiously along a newly-dug tunnel, picking their way over the chunks of rock that littered the floor.

Tyssan brought them to a halt by a narrow cleft. 'About a thousand yards along there, that side tunnel connects with the main shaft to the control area. It's the way I escaped myself.'

Commander Sharrel said, 'Lan, you will stay here and cover this exit. We may need to leave this place in a hurry.'

'Sir!' Lan stood to one side, and Commander Sharrel, the Doctor, Tyssan and Agella disappeared into the blackness of the tunnel. Lan was left alone. Drawing his blaster, he waited, poised and alert. The handsome, regular features showed not the slightest trace of fear . . . no trace of any emotion at all.

In the main cavern, a siren shattered the gloomy silence, and the prisoners collapsed thankfully beside their baskets. Now they would be given radiation pills, just enough food and drink to keep them alive, and allowed a few hours' exhausted sleep in the caves that served as dormitories, before the harsh voices of the Daleks awoke them, and drove them out to further toil.

'Work schedule now completed,' announced a

Dalek guard unnecessarily. 'Prisoners will return to detention area.' It moved over to the crumpled body of Romana, which had lain motionless and ignored since her collapse. 'Remove the body and dispose of it. Surface burial will be permitted.'

Two prisoners came forward with a rough wooden stretcher, and rolled Romana's body on to it.

'Help them.'

Two more prisoners came forward. The four of them hoisted the stretcher on to their shoulders and carried Romana's body away.

The Dalek leader saw a light flash on his monitoring console. He touched a control with his sucker-arm. 'Report.'

'Investigation of intruder in section seven so far without result.'

'Proceed with search and widen boundaries of search area. Advise me immediately of any results.'

'We obey.'

The Dalek moved away. The control area was left empty – but not for long.

The Doctor appeared at one of the entrances, looked round, then beckoned his companions onward. Commander Sharrel, Agella and Tyssan crept into the area after him. The little group stood looking about them.

'Well, Doctor, what now?' asked Commander Sharrel.

'Oh, we'll just poke about a bit,' said the Doctor vaguely. 'Never know what you'll find till you look.'

Commander Sharrel said, 'Agella, you cover the main entrance.'

Agella moved away to stand guard, and the others began their investigations.

The Doctor wandered around inquisitively, apparently fascinated by everything he saw. He opened a heavy metal cabinet and found it full of racks upon which lay stubby metal cylinders with timers set into their heads. 'Well, well,' said the Doctor. 'What have we here?'

Tyssan came over to him. 'Bombs, Doctor. Explosive charges with timers. Immensely powerful, too. They use them in the excavations.'

The Doctor nodded, and one of the bombs vanished into his capacious pocket. He moved on.

His eye was caught by the illuminated charts, and he crossed over to study them. 'Now this might tell us something. Interesting . . . very interesting indeed!'

Commander Sharrel came over to him. 'What are they, Doctor?'

'They seem to be plans of the old Kaled City.'

'Kaled?'

'Dalek, in another form. It would take too long to explain.' He pointed to the chart. 'This is the first underground level, where we are now. And here's the second. Presumably they've already penetrated at least that far.' He moved his finger down the chart. 'And here's level three . . . presumably this mark here represents their objective.' The Doctor pointed to a cross enclosed by a little circle.

'If that *is* their objective, what does the mark represent?'

'I have a very uneasy feeling about that,' said the Doctor, brooding. 'I wonder why the fourth level isn't marked?'

'The originals of these charts must be very old,' suggested Tyssan. 'Perhaps the plans for the fourth level were lost?'

'Possibly so. That would explain why they're drilling downwards. If only they knew it, they could reach the point they're after far more easily by gaining access to the fourth level and drilling *upwards.*'

The Doctor fished a pencil stub and a scrap of paper from his pocket and began drawing a rough map. 'Keep watch for me, will you, Tyssan? If this is the only plan of the city they've got, then there are quite a few things about this city that they don't know – and I do!'

Lan sensed movement further along the tunnel and ducked into the cleft, pressing himself against the wall.

A Dalek was moving along the main tunnel. It came closer . . . closer, and glided past, apparently without seeing him.

Lan waited a moment longer, then stepped into the tunnel, looking along it in the direction in which the Dalek had disappeared.

He heard a faint sound behind him and whirled round. A second Dalek had come silently up behind him. Lan raised his blaster, but before he could fire, the Dalek's gun-stick blazed. Lan writhed and twisted in the bright glow of the energy-discharge, and crumpled to the ground.

The first Dalek came back along the tunnel, and the two squat metallic shapes stared down at the motionless body.

The first Dalek said, 'Advise contol. Intruder has been located and exterminated.'

A steady bleep came from the communications console. The Doctor and his companions looked up in alarm. Surely the noise would summon a Dalek. At the same moment Agella called, 'Daleks, coming this way.'

'We'd better get out of here,' said the Doctor. He ran to the door by which they'd entered, then skidded to a halt. 'There's one coming this way too! Get under cover!'

All four ducked down behind a massive bank of equipment.

Two Daleks glided into the room, one through each entrance. The Dalek leader went over to answer the still bleeping console. 'Report!'

'Intruder located and exterminated. We are returning to control!'

The Doctor whispered, 'The place will be crawling with them in a minute. Let's make a run for it.'

He signalled to the others, who nodded assent. 'Now!' shouted the Doctor, and jumping from cover, he sprinted for the exit.

The Daleks reacted instantly, swinging round and opening fire. But by now the Doctor was already tearing along the corridor, the others at his heels.

From the control area behind them came the roar of Dalek blasters, and the shriek of angry Dalek voices. 'Alert! Alert! Intruders in control area. They must be found and exterminated!'

The Doctor and his group pelted down the main shaft and along the side tunnel, heading for the narrow cleft through which they'd entered. As they reached it, the Doctor stumbled over a huddled shape on the ground. Agella looked down. 'It is Lan,' she said emotionlessly.

'Let me have a look at him,' said the Doctor. 'Maybe I can help, I'm a doctor.'

With surprising strength, Agella held him back. 'No, Doctor. He is dead.'

'How can you be sure? At least let me look at him . . .'

Now Commander Sharrel moved to block his way. 'We are Movellans, Doctor. It is not permitted for aliens to see the bodies of our dead. It is against our code of honour . . .'

Commander Sharrel looked back down the tunnel. 'We must keep moving. The Daleks cannot be far behind us.'

The Doctor and Tyssan were politely but firmly urged past Lan's body. Only when they had both passed it, did the two Movellans follow them.

'What was all that about, Doctor?' muttered Tyssan.

'I don't know. But it would be terribly interesting to find out, wouldn't it?'

They hurried on their way, stumbling down the rubble-strewn tunnel back to the undergound chamber, where Tyssan's rope still dangled from the shaft.

'Up you go,' said the Doctor. 'Hurry!'

Tyssan began to climb, then hesitated. 'What about the girl, your friend? We were going to rescue her.'

'Don't worry, we'll find her,' said the Doctor confidently. 'We haven't finished here yet.'

Tyssan vanished up the shaft, and the Doctor

waved to the Movellans to go next. 'After you.'

'No, Doctor, after you,' said Commander Sharrel evenly.

'How kind!'

The Doctor shinned nimbly up the rope, and the Movellans followed.

Three Daleks glided down the tunnel, past Lan's huddled body and through the archway into the underground chamber.

Guns blazing, they raked the chamber with a deadly burst of fire. But the chamber was empty. They moved across the room and directed their fire up the shaft . . .

There was a slithering sound and a coil of rope slid down the shaft and dropped in front of them. The Doctor's voice floated down. 'Think you're the most superior race in the Universe, don't you? Well, just try climbing up after us!'

The Dalek patrol leader said, 'Guard this position. We shall report to control.'

Two of the Daleks moved away. The third stayed at the bottom of the shaft, eye-stalk peering upwards for the enemies it could no longer reach.

The Doctor, Tyssan and the two surviving Movellans hurried out of the ruined building and across the plain. As they reached the open space, the Doctor paused in sudden horror. The burial mound he had investigated was still there. Now there was a second mound beside it.

A terrible fear came into the Doctor's mind. 'Oh no! Not Romana!' Feverishly he began pulling rocks away from the mound.

The Secret of the Daleks

The Doctor worked frantically, desperate to uncover the body, dreading what he might find – and realised that there *was* no body, just a hollow space in the centre of the mound.

A voice behind him said, 'Looking for somebody, Doctor?'

The Doctor turned. Romana was standing beside him, tired and ill-looking, covered with the ever-present grey dust, but unmistakably alive.

The Doctor jumped up and gave her a hug of welcome. 'Romana! Do you know, for a moment I thought . . .'

' – that it was my burial mound? Well, it was, actually! The only way to escape from the Daleks was to die, so that's what I did! Luckily they didn't realise I was from Gallifrey.'

The Doctor patted her on the back. 'Good girl!'

By now the others had come up and the Doctor introduced Romana. 'What's being from Gallifrey got to do with dying and coming to life again?' demanded Tyssan.

'I was taught at school how to suspend my breathing and stop my hearts.'

'Hearts? How many have you got then?'

'Two! One for everyday, and one for best!'

The Doctor had taken his map from his pocket and was studying it absorbedly. Suddenly he dashed towards a ruined building.

'Doctor, where are you going?' called Romana.

'Dalek hunting,' said the Doctor grimly, and disappeared inside the building.

When the others caught up with him he was heaving at a pile of rubble in the far corner of the room. 'If I'm right, there should be a shaftway that the Daleks don't know about leading straight down to the bottom level.'

They helped him to pull away the rocks, and a few minutes' hard work revealed a rusty iron door. The Doctor grabbed the handle and heaved. With a protesting, rusty creak the door swung open.

'There,' said the Doctor triumphantly. 'Now, if the Daleks are looking for what I think they're looking for, we've got a chance to get there first!' He turned to the two Movellans. 'No need for us all to go. Why don't you two go back to your ship and wait for us?'

Commander Sharrel considered this with his usual calm deliberation. 'No. I will go back to the ship – I may be needed. Agella will go with you. We are just as anxious to find what the Daleks are looking for as you are, Doctor. Stay in touch, Agella.'

The Movellan girl nodded gravely. 'Of course, Commander.'

Commander Sharrel turned and strode unhurriedly away.

'Wait a moment,' said Tyssan. 'We'll need this.' He produced a resin torch from a hiding place in the corner, and lit it with a flame-device from his pouch. 'I brought this with me when I escaped.'

'Come on then,' said the Doctor, and led the way through the door, and down the steeply descending passageway beyond.

It was a long and tiring journey, down and down

into the ruined catacombs of the deepest level of the city. The flickering light of the torch showed them long crumbling corridors, littered with rubble and festooned with cobwebs. They passed gloomy cellars and storage areas, rusting power plants filled with long-silent machines. Often their way was blocked by rockfalls and they had to set to work to clear a passage for themselves.

After they had forced their way through the latest of these obstacles, the Doctor sat down on a chunk of masonry and mopped his brow. 'We're nearly there now. We can afford to rest for a minute or two.'

Wearily the others all sat down. All except Agella, who seemed as fresh and untired as when they had set off. Romana noticed enviously that she wasn't even out of breath.

'Are you sure you know where we're going, Doctor?' asked Tyssan. 'How did you know how to get down to this level?'

'Call it local knowledge – gained a very long time ago. I made a study of this city once. Romana, isn't it time you took some more of those pills?'

'I've already had six,' protested Romana. 'I'm all right now, Doctor, honestly.'

'Well, I hope so. You gave me a nasty turn up there. You and your burial mound!'

Romana smiled, rather pleased that the Doctor had been so concerned for her.

Suddenly they heard the familiar sound of drilling. It seemed to come from somewhere above them, somewhere very close.

'They've started up again,' said the Doctor. 'We may not have much time.'

'What are we looking for?' asked Romana.

'The same thing as the Daleks.'

'And what's that?'

'I'll tell you when I'm sure. Frankly, I almost hope I'm wrong.' The Doctor sighed. 'Unfortunately, I very seldom am. This way!' Picking up the torch, he led them into the darkness.

The Dalek leader swung round as a guard came into control. 'Report!'

'Combat units continuing extensive search. No result as yet.'

'Hostiles must be located. Order all patrols. Seek, locate, exterminate!'

'I obey.'

The guard moved away, and a Dalek engineer came forward.

Again the Dalek leader grated, 'Report!'

'Drilling has recommenced. Computer predicts penetration into objective area now imminent.'

The Dalek leader turned to the communications technician. 'Advise Space Fleet Command that our mission is almost complete.' The Dalek leader moved over to the map, focusing its eye-stalk on the sign that marked the objective – a cross enclosed in a circle.

The Doctor led the way into yet another underground chamber. It was huge and cavernous, littered with rubble and thick with cobwebs. Time-rusted instrument banks stood around the room. It looked as if the place might have been a laboratory, or perhaps some kind of command centre.

The Doctor held up the torch and looked round. 'Unless I'm mistaken, what we're looking for should be somewhere around here.'

He moved over to a corner which seemed to be walled of by an incredibly dense curtain of spider's web.

The Doctor parted the web with his hands, tearing aside the clinging folds. 'Yes, just as I thought.'

'What is it, Doctor?' asked Romana.

The Doctor held up the torch.

Romana saw a man, slumped back in a kind of elaborate wheelchair. Or at least, something that had once been a man. The withered old body was wrapped in a high-collared plastic coverall, and surrounded by what looked like an astonishing variety of life-support systems. Only one hand was visible, a withered claw poised over a set of controls built into the wide arm of the chair.

The face was the most horrifying thing of all. Parchment-thin skin clung to a shrivelled skull, the eyes were sunken pits, the mouth a thin, cruel gash. Wires and plastic tubes formed a helmet-like arrangement suspended over the head. Even in life, the man could have been only barely alive, thought Romana. Lungs, heart, speech, hearing, sight – *everything* must have been mechanically or electronically aided. The creature was more machine than man.

The others crowded forward to look.

'Who was it?' whispered Agella.

'Davros. The evil genius who first created the Daleks.'

'*He* created the Daleks? A humanoid?'

'Yes – and I could have stopped him.'

'You? How could you?' said Tyssan in astonishment. 'This – *thing's* been dead for centuries.'

'I know. Curious the tricks that time can play.'

Agella said, 'And *that* is what the Daleks are looking for? This humanoid, their creator. But why? What do they need – ?'

There was a rumble, a roaring crash, and Agella vanished beneath a pile of rubble. A huge chunk of ceiling had caved in directly on top of her. When the dust cleared Agella had almost completely disappeared. Only one hand could still be seen, jutting pathetically from a huge pile of rocks.

Coughing and choking, the Doctor hurried over, grasping the hand in a vain attempt to pull her free.

Suddenly he stopped, examining the hand in astonishment. 'So, that's why . . .' he muttered.

There was more rumbling, the hole in the ceiling widened and rocks and loose rubble rained down upon them.

'It's the Daleks,' shouted Tyssan. 'They're breaking through.'

The Doctor, Romana and Tyssan peered upwards through the dust-filled air.

They failed to notice that something was happening to the figure in the chair behind them.

The slumped body suddenly became more erect.

The fingers flexed, scrabbling on the arm of the chair.

The head lifted, the mouth writhed and the eyes opened. Davros was coming to life.

8

The Prisoner

They heard a creak of movement, and turned.

Davros, now fully alive again, was edging towards them in his wheelchair. He spoke in a voice dry and creaking from long disuse. 'So, the long darkness has ended, the eternity of waiting has finished. The resurrection has come as I always knew it would.'

'You must forgive me if I seem less than overjoyed by your revival,' said the Doctor dryly. 'Frankly, I'd rather hoped that you were dead.'

'Dead?' said Davros scornfully. 'Gods do not die! Mark this moment in your minds . . . In all the history of the Universe, this instant of time is unique. Davros lives!'

'I can see your long rest has done nothing to cure your megalomania,' began the Doctor.

A tremendous rumbling crash from the darkness behind them interrupted him. There was a roar of falling masonry, and a sudden silence. 'They've stopped drilling,' whispered Tyssan.

The Doctor said, 'Yes— so they've probably broken through!'

The Dalek leader was waiting impatiently for news. One of his aides glided forward. 'Entry to level four has now been cleared.'

'Excellent. All units will proceed to area four

immediately. Anti-gravitational discs will be issued.'
'I obey.'

From all over the base, Daleks converged upon level
four. Floating down through the gap from level three
on their eerily silent anti-grav discs, the advance
patrol reached the spot they had been seeking for so
long— Davros's underground control room.

It was empty.

The patrol leader said, 'Charts indicate objective
located in this precise position. Scan the area.'

The Daleks began sweeping to and fro, and soon
one of them reported, 'Surface disturbance. Humanoid
footprints!' The Daleks scanned the floor with their
incredibly sensitive eye-lenses. In the thick dust of
the floor, they registered footprints leading away,
beside them the wheel-marks of Davros's chair.

'Follow!' ordered the patrol leader. 'Follow!
Follow! Follow!'

The other Daleks hurried away. The patrol leader
signalled, 'All units full alert. Emergency!
Emergency! Emergency!'

The Doctor led the way rapidly along a gloomy
corridor, his torch held high. He seemed to have an
unerring sense of direction, and took one turning
after another without hesitation. Tyssan and Romana
hurried after him, pushing Davros's chair between
them. Romana realised that the Doctor was simply
taking the corridors that seemed to slope upwards,
concerned only to get them to the surface.

Davros didn't seem to be enjoying the trip. 'You

will release me,' he screeched. 'You will return me to the Daleks.'

'You be quiet or I'll switch you off,' warned the Doctor. They hurried on. They reached a junction, the Doctor turned left, and suddenly stopped. A patrol of Daleks was gliding past the other end of the corridor.

'Back this way,' he whispered, and they turned in the other direction.

The nightmare journey went on and on. They roamed through the endless corridors heading always for the surface. Eventually, they found a long ramp which wound around and around, in a rapidly ascending spiral. 'Up we go,' said the Doctor, and leant a hand with Davros's chair.

It was agonising work heaving the chair up the steep incline but they struggled on, passing first one and then another exit from the ramp. 'That was the third and second level,' grunted the Doctor. 'The next should be first.'

The spiral ramp ended at last, opening out into a long corridor. The Doctor bustled them along it. 'We should be on the surface level by now. All we need to do is find a way out.'

The corridor led into a hallway and at the end of the hall was a set of rusting iron doors, partly blocked by rubble. The doors were warped and twisted with age, and just above the top of them was a gleam of daylight.

'You keep watch behind us, Tyssan. Come on, Romana, let's try to clear that doorway.'

The Doctor studied the pile of rubble. 'Most of it seems to be supported by this beam here. If we can shift that . . .' He shoved hard on the beam which seemed to shift a little. 'Come on, Romana, give me a hand.'

They put their shoulders to the beam and shoved. 'It's going,' said the Doctor exultantly. 'It's shifting . . .'

A final heave and the beam came free. The pile of rubble collapsed in a cloud of dust. Unfortunately, the vibration disturbed an already weakened ceiling, and an even bigger pile of rubble thundered down, burying the remains of the first – and blocking the door completely.

'I'm afraid we didn't do that very well,' said the Doctor sadly.

Tyssan came running back towards them. 'Daleks – at the other end of the corridor.'

'We seem to be boxed in,' said the Doctor thoughtfully. He looked round. 'It's too exposed here. Let's get under cover.'

The only cover available was a small room, set just to one side of the blocked gates, and the Doctor led them into it.

The room was small and bare. The buckled metal door had fallen from rusted hinges and lay just to one side of the doorway. The only useful feature was a long narrow transom window set high in the far wall. Daylight shone through shattered panes of glass.

'See if you can prop that door back up,' ordered the Doctor. 'Try and make some kind of barricade.' He climbed on a pile of rubble and peered through the window.

Ahead of him stretched the usual Skaro landscape, an endless rubble-strewn plain, broken up by scattered clumps of ruined buildings.

The Doctor jumped down and went to help Romana and Tyssan. Between them they managed to heave the door back into place, propping it up with a kind of rough wall, built from broken masonry.

Davros looked on from his chair with a disdainful sneer.

Romana straightened up, and rubbed her aching back. 'Well, that's the best we can manage, Doctor – and it wouldn't keep out a determined mouse.'

'It will have to do,' said the Doctor grimly. 'Now listen to me carefully you two. I want you both to get out through that window and make your way to the Movellan space ship. Tell them to organise a force and mount an attack at this point. It's vital that we get Davros away from here before the Daleks find him.'

'What about you?'

The Doctor looked at the long narrow window. 'Well, I could get out but we'd never get him through.' He nodded towards Davros. 'I'll just have to stay here and see the Daleks don't get him.'

'We can't just leave you here,' protested Romana.

'Your loyalty is very touching,' said the Doctor briskly, 'but not very practical. Just do as I say, please.' Romana opened her mouth to argue and the Doctor said, 'If there's one thing I hate it's people who use age and rank to enforce their will – so don't make me do it! No more arguments, please!'

The Doctor nodded to Tyssan who climbed up the rubble and began squeezing carefully through the narrow gap.

'All right, Doctor,' said Romana. 'Have it your own way. We'll be as quick as we can. Don't take unnecessary chances, will you?'

'Only necessary ones,' promised the Doctor solemnly. 'If the Daleks don't bother me, I won't bother them. Now, off you go!'

He helped Romana up the pile. She squeezed through the window and dropped to the ground below, where Tyssan was waiting.

With a farewell wave at the window, Tyssan and Romana turned and hurried away.

The Doctor climbed the pile and watched them vanish into the distance.

He jumped down, and peered through the gap in the barricade. The hall beyond was silent and deserted.

He turned back to Davros. 'Well, now we have a little time to ourselves, I can fill you in on some of the more important events that have taken place during the centuries you've been resting. Now let me see . . . Earth won the Intergalactic Olympic Games . . . Betelguese came to a close second. The economy of Algol is in a terrible state, galloping inflation, you know . . .'

The harsh rusty voice of Davros cut across the Doctor's flow of chatter. 'Do you really believe your puny efforts can change the course of my destiny?'

'Let's just say that I hope to tamper with it a little.'

The Doctor fished in his pocket, and produced the stubby explosive canister. He fished out his sonic screwdriver, and began dismantling the cylinder, like a man doing some minor task just to pass the time.

Davros launched into a long ranting speech. 'Destiny, Doctor. Destiny! Irrevocable, predetermined events. Power that fore-ordains more power. *My* power. *My* invincibility. *My* supreme plan to control the Universe.'

'Yes, yes, I've heard all that before,' said the Doctor patiently. 'Now do keep quiet, there's a good chap. I've got a tricky little job on here and I need to concentrate.'

66

But there was no hope of stopping Davros now. Deprived of an audience for centuries, he was making the most of this opportunity.

'The errors of the past will be rectified. I will add new design elements to the Dalek circuitry. Points that are now vulnerable will be made invulnerable. The Daleks will be armed with new, more powerful weapons, so devastating that all will succumb to them. I will equip them with computer circuits that will hold all the knowledge of the Universe. I will – '

The Doctor looked up. 'Why bother? The Daleks can do all that perfectly well for themselves.'

'I am their creator. The Daleks need me!'

'The Daleks outgrew their need for you centuries ago. You'd already given them everything they needed, the potential to develop, to grow in evil. That's why they turned on you, left you for dead.' He looked thoughtfully at Davros. 'So why have they come back here for you now, eh? What special circumstances have made the Daleks think they need *your* help again?'

Davros had nothing to say.

Commander Sharrel sat in his chair, studying a flow of images across a screen. He saw the tunnels, the pursuing Daleks . . . and he saw Davros. The last image in the sequence was of an obliterating shower of rubble and the screen went blank. The images had been transmitted through Agella's eyes.

Sharrel addressed his crew. 'The Daleks have gained their objective.'

The picture of Davros appeared on the screen. 'Name: Davros. History: creator of the Dalek species, humanoid, crippled, dependent on sophisticated life-support system, possibly mutant through massive overdoses of radiation. These data will now be processed so that future strategy may be determined.'

A Dalek scout moved cautiously across the hall. The trail was wide, impossible to lose. Humanoid footprints and the wheel-marks of Davros's chair.

The tracks led straight to a door, which appeared to be blocked by some kind of barricade.

The Dalek waited. From beyond the barricade it could hear the low drone of voices.

Switching its aural circuits to maximum receptivity, the Dalek slid forward.

It listened for a moment longer, then turned and moved swiftly away.

The objective had been found.

Tyssan and Romana hurried swiftly across the plain. 'How much longer?' gasped Romana.

Tyssan paused. 'Well, if I've got my bearings correctly, the Movellan ship should be just on the other side of the rise. Not long now.'

They moved on, to a point where the rough track they were following skirted the side of a ruined building. Tyssan peered round the corner and came to a sudden halt. 'Daleks! Two of them guarding the path.'

'What do we do now?'

'Well, we could go back, work our way round the bottom of the rise.'

'How long would it take?'

Tyssan shrugged. 'Hard to say. Put another hour on the journey, maybe more.'

Romana thought of the Doctor, alone behind the flimsy barricade, trying to guard his captive from the eagerly searching Daleks. 'We can't afford any delay. It's only a matter of time before the Daleks find the Doctor. We've got to get help to him as soon as we can.'

Tyssan said, 'All right. You see those ruins?' He pointed to a half-destroyed building just to one side of the track. 'You get under cover. I'll let the Daleks see me, and try to lead them away.'

'I can't let you, Tyssan. It's too dangerous.'

'There's no alternative, is there? As you said yourself, we can't afford the delay. If I manage to get away from them, I'll follow you to the ship as soon as I can.'

Romana nodded, accepting Tyssan's logic. 'Good luck,' she said and ran to the ruins. She watched Tyssan walk boldly around the corner of the building and stand waiting. Presumably he was now in full view of the Daleks, though Romana couldn't see them from her hiding place. For a long moment, nothing happened . . .

Tyssan stood watching the two Daleks as they patrolled up and down. His mind was full of his own gloomy prophecy, that he was destined to die on Skaro.

The nearest Dalek suddenly spotted Tyssan. Its gun-arm came up, and a chunk of wall close to his head exploded in flames.

Tyssan turned and ran.

With appalling speed, the Daleks glided after him, firing as they came.

9

The Hostages

Tyssan weaved and ducked as he ran. All around him the rocky ground exploded in great bursts of smoke and flame.

Romana saw him flash past, the two Daleks close behind him, their gun-sticks blazing.

Tyssan tripped and fell, disappearing behind a boulder. A Dalek scored a direct hit, and the boulder exploded in smoke and flame. Somehow Tyssan managed to scramble to his feet and keep on running.

He bounded down the slope in enormous strides, and the Daleks sped after him.

Romana jumped out of her hiding place and began running frantically for the Movellan ship.

The Doctor finished his work on the canister, and returned the sonic screwdriver to his pocket. 'There, that should do nicely.'

Davros's curiosity overcame him. 'What is the purpose of that device, Doctor?'

'Life insurance! Now, what shall we talk about to pass the time?'

'Your approaching and inevitable destruction?'

'No. We had that conversation the last time we met. I'm more interested in your survival than my destruction. I *saw* you destroyed, the Daleks blasted you from point blank range.'

There was satisfaction in Davros's voice. 'I had suspected the possibility of treachery for some time, and I had prepared a shielding-device. Its circuits were burnt out by blaster fire, but it served its purpose. Even so, there was damage to my primary life-support system. Secondary and back-up circuits switched on immediately. Synthetic tissue regeneration took place automatically, while bodily organs were held in suspension.'

The Doctor shook his head, marvelling at the lunatic ingenuity with which Davros had ensured his own survival. 'You know, I'd say you've really outstayed your welcome in a big way! Talk about not taking a hint!'

'Until the universal supremacy of the Daleks is fully established, I cannot permit myself the luxury of death,' said Davros grandly. 'It is, however, a luxury I shall take the greatest pleasure in bestowing on you, Doctor.'

'What a splendidly generous chap you are!'

An almost wistful note came into Davros's voice. 'Since my entombment, I have had no knowledge of the advancement of my Daleks. Tell me, Doctor, they have achieved much?'

'Oh, yes,' said the Doctor grimly. 'They've spread havoc and destruction throughout the ten galaxies, destroyed countless innocent lives. They're like the viruses that carry plague and pestilence. Your Daleks are no better than annoying little bugs, Davros. One day they'll be stamped out altogether.'

Davros smiled. 'As yet, you have seen only the beginning! Now I have returned, the Dalek campaign of conquest will begin in earnest. I have slept, but now I have awakened, and soon the Universe will be sorry.'

'You're misquoting poor old Napoleon,' said the Doctor scornfully. 'Remind me to tell you what happened to him some time.'

Davros went ranting on. 'Armed with new technology, we shall conquer and destroy . . .'

The Doctor lost patience. 'Oh, shut up, Davros! Just you sit and do a bit of silent brooding, there's a good fellow.'

Davros fell silent, a malignant smile on his lips. The Doctor's nerve was beginning to crack.

The Doctor jumped up to look out of the window. The plain was empty, no sign of the Movellans, blasters in their hands, dashing to the rescue like the US Cavalry. Come to think of it, the Doctor was beginning to feel uncomfortably like General Custer. Impatient chap, Custer, never listened to his warnings . . .

The Doctor's rambling reflections were interrupted by a colossal explosion. The centre of his barracade disintegrated in smoke and flame.

The Daleks had arrived.

The Doctor leaped to one side of the door, flattening himself against the wall, and peered cautiously through the clouds of smoke.

A line of Daleks was assembled in front of the door. Their leader glided forward. 'You will move out into the open. If you fail to obey in five seconds, you will be exterminated.' The Dalek began to count. 'One . . . two . . . three . . .'

The Doctor shot across the room and crouched down behind Davros's chair.

The Dalek voice came through the doorway. 'Four . . .'

'I should stop the countdown right there if I were

72

you,' yelled the Doctor. He shook the chair a little. 'Tell them what I've got here, Davros. Tell them!'

'He is holding a primed explosive device,' called Davros.

'That's right,' shouted the Doctor. 'One move and it's going off, right down the back of his chair. It will turn Davros and his life support systems into so much scrap metal. Now, back away, all of you.'

'Do as he says,' called Davros. 'He seeks only to buy a little time.'

There was a long pause. Then the Dalek leader grated, 'We obey.'

The line of Daleks receded, but not very far.

The Doctor heaved a sigh of relief. 'This, I believe, is what is known on the planet Earth as a Mexican stand-off!'

'Only for the moment,' said Davros calmly. 'How long do you think you can sustain your advantage alone and against such odds?'

'Wouldn't you like to know,' said the Doctor mockingly.

He sneaked a quick glance up at the transom and muttered, 'Come to that, wouldn't *I* like to know?'

The waiting continued, and the seconds creaked slowly by.

Romana struggled up to the Movellan space ship, slipped past the sentry at the ramp, hurried into the control room, and promptly collapsed.

Commander Sharrel came hurrying over, and two of his crew lifted Romana on to a couch.

'What is it? What happened?'

'The Doctor needs help. He's hiding out in a small

room in the City . . .' Romana broke off as she saw the picture of Davros on the screen. 'Where did you get that? How can you know about Davros already?'

'We have our methods,' said Commander Sharrel impassively. He turned to a crewman. 'Get an armed patrol together immediately. Set off as soon as you're ready to move out.'

Members of the crew began taking blasters from wall-racks and assembling by the exit ramp.

Romana tried to get up. 'I must go with them.'

Commander Sharrel pressed her back in her chair. 'No, you must rest. You have done your part. We shall take care of things now.'

'Thank you,' said Romana weakly. She slumped back in her chair. 'You'll hurry though, won't you? The Doctor is in great danger.'

'Tell my crewmen where to find him,' said Commander Sharrel, and Romana gave directions to the place where the Doctor was hiding. Commander Sharrel gave orders, and the patrol moved out.

Romana was fascinated by the picture of Davros.

Commander Sharrel caught the direction of her glance. He leaned forward and switched off the screen.

The Doctor, crouched down behind Davros's chair, was getting cramp. The Daleks had been silent for some time, though the Doctor had heard a bustle of movement, shouted orders and strangely enough, what sounded like human voices.

Suddenly the voice of the Dalek leader blared out. 'Attention! Attention! The action we are about to take is your responsibility. It will continue until you agree to total surrender.'

'Action? What action?' thought the Doctor irritably. Did they mean they were going to open fire again? And in that case, why bother to warn him? He shifted position, raising his head so that he could see through the gap in the ruined barricade. A little group of slave workers was huddled just to one side of the door, guarded by a ring of Daleks.

The Dalek leader pointed. 'You come forward.'

A prisoner was thrust forward to stand in front of the door.

'Exterminate!' Two of the Dalek guards opened fire. The prisoner twisted in the glow of their weapons, and then fell dead to the ground. Another prisoner was thrust forward. 'Exterminate!'

The Daleks fired again, and the second man died like the first.

A third prisoner was thrust forward, this time a young girl.

The Doctor jumped up. 'Stop!' he shouted. 'Stop it!'

The Dalek leader moved forward. 'Do you agree to surrender?'

'I'll agree to let you have Davros – but only under my conditions.'

'State them.'

'All slave workers are to be released immediately, and allowed to leave the city.'

'Continue.'

'Nobody will enter this room until I'm away and clear.'

'Unacceptable. Exterminations will continue.' The guards trained their weapons on the prisoner.

'Wait,' shouted the Doctor. 'One more killing and I'll detonate the charge. If you kill another prisoner, then I'll kill Davros.'

The Dalek considered. 'Logic unacceptable. Detonation of device would also destroy you.'

'I know that – and I don't care. You hadn't foreseen that one, had you?'

'Self-sacrifice – illogical, therefore impossible,' said the Dalek leader. 'Exterminations will continue.'

The Doctor raised the bomb.

'Agree!' shrieked Davros. 'Agree to his terms. He will do what he says. He is humanoid. Their logic is impaired by irrational sentiment. Agree to his terms. I, Davros, command it!'

There was another long pause.

Then came the voice of the Dalek leader. 'We obey.'

The Doctor peered over the barricade. He saw the Dalek guards draw back, and the astonished prisoners urged away. Scarcely able to believe their luck, they turned and ran.

The Dalek leader called, 'The prisoners have been released.'

The Doctor stood up. 'All right. I still need some time to get clear.' He wedged the explosive canister down the back of the chair, and then held his sonic screwdriver in front of Davros. 'I told you that bomb was my life insurance. I've adapted it so it can be detonated by remote control. All I have to do is press this switch and – boom!'

'You need not elaborate, Doctor.'

'Just as long as you understand.' The Doctor climbed up to the window. 'I'd like to say it has been nice to renew old acquaintance, but I'm afraid . . .'

'We'll meet again, Doctor,' called Davros, 'never doubt it – we'll meet again.'

The Doctor disappeared through the window.

Davros began scrabbling frantically for the bomb, with his one good arm. He was unable to reach it. He headed his chair towards the doorway, rushing to meet the advancing Daleks. 'The explosive! Remove it! Quickly – the Doctor will detonate! Remove the bomb!'

The Doctor sprinted across the plain, pausing when he was a safe distance away. He looked back at the building he had left.

He looked at his sonic screwdriver, as if troubled by the action he must take.

The Doctor sighed. He had hesitated once before, at a time when he could have destroyed the Daleks before their creation, simply by touching the two wires that would complete an explosive circuit. Who knows what horrors he had unleashed upon the Universe? The Daleks were stronger now and more numerous, and with Davros to help them . . . He must not hesitate again.

The Doctor pressed the switch.

10

The Bait

Davros shot out into the hallway. 'Remove the canister,' he shrieked. 'Remove the canister. It is wedged at the back of my chair!'

Two Daleks came forward. Under Davros's frenzied directions, they managed to locate the canister with their sucker-arms and remove it.

'Away!' shouted Davros. 'Remove the canister immediately!'

Obediently the two Dalek guards moved to the far end of the long hall, the canister held between them.

At that moment, the Doctor pressed the switch.

There was an intense, localised explosion. Both Daleks burst into flame.

From the other end of the hall, Davros watched them burn. He turned his chair towards the Dalek leader. 'Come, there is much to be done. You must tell me of all the Dalek victories that have been won whilst I have slept . . . and of all the defeats. I shall learn from your mistakes. The Daleks shall be made into perfect creatures, they will be invincible. The Daleks will rule the Universe.'

Followed by his retinue of Daleks, Davros glided away.

No one spared a glance for the two sacrificed Daleks, burning at the end of the hall.

Davros lived. That was all that mattered.

Romana sat talking to Commander Sharrel, who was showing a flattering interest in her account of the Doctor's history and accomplishments.

'I don't suppose there's anyone living who knows more about the Daleks than the Doctor. He's studied them for years, he knows how they work, how they act, how they think. But then, of course, he's an absolute genius at robotics . . .' Romana stopped herself, thinking it was just as well the Doctor wasn't there. He was quite conceited enough already. 'We can't just sit here talking. What's happening to that patrol of yours?'

'When they find him they will report. There is no news yet.'

Romana stood up. 'I think I'll go and see if I can help. Perhaps they haven't been able to find him.'

Commander Sharrel took her arm and pushed her gently back in her seat. 'No. You will be safer here.'

'I don't care about being safe. I want to know what's happened to the Doctor.'

'You will stay here.'

There was something menacing in the flat, calm voice, and suddenly Romana was frightened. 'Get your hands off me! I'm leaving – now!'

She jumped to her feet and managed to pull free of his grip. Two Movellans appeared behind her, and Commander Sharrel snapped, 'Hold her.'

Romana swung round, looked at the faces of the Movellans, and caught her breath in horror.

Lan and Agella were standing before her. Lan had been blasted down by the Daleks, Agella had died under a crushing rock fall. But they were here, both of them.

Romana backed away. 'You're dead,' she whispered. 'You were killed . . .'

Agella took Romana's arm, touched the muzzle of her gun to her neck and fired. There was an electronic buzz, and Romana fell to the ground.

'I used emission level three, Commander,' said Agella calmly. 'Consciousness will not return for some time.'

'Good. Now, listen to me both of you. Up till now, our aim has been simply to discover the objective of the Daleks in coming to this planet. Whatever that objective was, our intention was to take it from the Daleks, in the hope that it would be of equal value to us.' Commander Sharrel paused. 'Now we know that the objective is Davros – and Davros will never agree to serve the Movellans. Davros is useless to us, and our aim must simply be to destroy him.' He turned to Lan. 'You will prepare the Nova Device for surface testing. We will use it to destroy this planet – as soon as we have secured our new objective.'

Agella was puzzled. 'But if our objective is not Davros . . .'

Commander Sharrel switched on the read-out screen. A new picture replaced Davros on the screen, the picture of a tall man with a long scarf, and a battered wide-brimmed hat jammed on to a tangle of curly hair.

'There is our new objective,' said Commander Sharrel. 'The Doctor!'

Unaware of this flattering demand for his services, the Doctor was lying perfectly still in an uncomfortably narrow rocky crevice, hoping two patrolling Daleks would pass by him.

His position was complicated by the fact that one

of Skaro's nastier life-forms was crawling up his arm. It was a pulsating green blob, a kind of land-jellyfish, and the Doctor was hoping very hard that it wasn't carnivorous. As it inched its way along his arm towards his shoulder, the Doctor wondered how long he was going to be able to keep still if it reached his face.

The blob surmounted the Doctor's shoulder, and headed for his ear – just as the two Daleks disappeared from sight behind some ruins. The Doctor leaped to his feet, scooped the creature from his shoulder, and dropped it gently back into the crevice.

'There you go, old chap,' murmured the Doctor. 'Some kind of Kaled mutant species presumably . . . and the Daleks were originally mutated Kaleds themselves!'He tipped his hat to the blob, which was crawling rapidly back into its crevice. 'Thank you very much, my dear chap. I think you've just told me why the Daleks need Davros!'

A shadow fell over the Doctor. Someone had crept quietly up behind him.

The Doctor spun round in alarm – and smiled, as he saw Tyssan looking down at him. He jumped to his feet and held out his hand. 'Tyssan! What are you doing here?'

'Looking for you, amongst other things.' Tyssan gave a brief account of his escape with Romana, and of the way he'd drawn off the Daleks. 'I managed to get away from them in the end. I've been trying to work my way back to the space ship. It's dangerous to move around though, there are Dalek patrols everywhere.'

'So I've noticed,' said the Doctor ruefully. 'We

seem to have stirred them up rather, don't we?'

'I ran into some of the freed prisoners. They told me what you'd done for them, and they're very grateful.'

'Where are they now?'

'In hiding, most of them. They've managed to steal some supplies. If I could get hold of some decent weapons, we could turn them into some kind of fighting force.'

'That could be useful. Maybe you'd better take me to see them – '

A metallic, grating voice interrupted them. 'Stay where you are.'

The Doctor and Tyssan turned.

A Dalek was behind them covering them with its gun-arm at point blank range.

'You will turn and walk ahead of me. If you attempt to escape you will be exterminated. Move!'

The Doctor and Tyssan looked at each other, gauging the chances of resistance.

'Move!' screeched the Dalek. It was obvious that it would blast them at the slightest excuse.

The Doctor shrugged, and both men started walking towards the Dalek.

Suddenly there was the roar of a heavy blaster from somewhere above them. The Dalek exploded like a roman candle, sending up a fountain of flame.

The Doctor looked upwards. A Movellan stood on a rock, overlooking the track, blaster in hand.

The Movellan jumped down, and came towards them. 'That was very decent of you,' said the Doctor. 'We really are awfully grateful . . .' The Movellan's blaster was aimed straight at the Doctor.

'You will accompany me to the space craft.'

'All in good time, old chap. I've some people to see first.'

'That was not a request, Doctor, it was an order. Move.'

'I seem to be in considerable demand today!'

The Doctor walked up to the Movellan, then suddenly stumbled on a piece of rock. He fell against the Movellan, grabbed at him to steady himself – and snatched the shining metal tube from the Movellan's belt.

The Movellan staggered and dropped his gun. His movements became slow and unco-ordinated. He flailed helplessly about and then collapsed.

For a moment he lay twitching on the ground, like a beetle on its back, then lay still.

Tyssan looked on in astonishment. 'What's happening, Doctor? Why have the Movellans suddenly turned against you?'

'I'm not all that sure they were ever for me. Let's take a look at this chap. If my theory is correct . . .'

The Doctor knelt beside the Movellan and opened his tunic. He gave a grunt of satisfaction. 'Just as I thought. Look!' Tyssan stared in amazement. The Movellan's chest seemed to be made not of flesh and blood but of metal. The Doctor slid back a panel to reveal a metal cavity packed with electronic circuitry. 'A robot race, you see. Not so very different from the Daleks. You know, there's a way we could find the Movellans very useful.' The Doctor opened out the silver tube and studied the circuits within. 'Take a look at this, Tyssan . . .'

Not far away, a small party of Movellans was setting

up a scientific device. It consisted of a small metal box with controls set into the lid. The box was being inserted into a transparent container, rather like a giant test-tube.

Lan checked that the device was properly seated and then fastened the seals.

He addressed the other crew members. 'Most of you are not yet familiar with the Nova Device. It is one of the latest triumphs of Movellan technology. I shall explain its operation. The Device changes the molecular structure of planetary atmosphere, rendering the very air flammable. The molecules are ignited by a small but intense explosion, and a chain reaction is set up.' Lan paused impressively. 'We are about to test the Device within a protective shield. If we were to detonate without that shield, as we shall do once we have left this planet, the entire surface atmosphere would burst into flame, reducing the whole planet to a blazing cinder.'

He flicked a control in the base of the Device. 'Stand back.'

The Movellans withdrew and waited.

A few seconds later, a blinding white flash filled the interior of the plastic shielding. The container gave out a blaze of white-hot light, too powerful for the naked eye to look at. Lan nodded in satisfaction. The Device had functioned perfectly.

Agella looked up from a communications console. 'Lan reports that the Nova Device is ready.'

'That is excellent news,' said Commander Sharrel. 'Unfortunately, our patrols have not yet succeeded in finding the Doctor. The patrol sent to rescue him found that he had already gone. They were forced to fall back under heavy Dalek attack. In addition, another crewman has vanished. We need some way to force the Doctor out into the open.' He looked at Romana, unconscious in her chair. 'And I think I know how that can be done . . .'

The Doctor decided he would go to the Movellan space ship after all, not as a prisoner, but of his own free will. Whatever the true nature of the Movellans, he was still allied to them by mutual opposition to the Daleks. The Doctor reckoned it ought to be possible to come to some kind of agreement. After all, he had nothing against robots . . .

The Doctor and Tyssan came over the rise that led to the Movellan space ship, and stopped in amazement.

The Nova Device had been set up just in front of them. Romana was inside the protective casing, the detonating box at her feet.

The Doctor ran up to the Device. He wasn't entirely sure of its purpose, but it was clear enough that the box was some kind of bomb. He could even see a timing device ticking away the seconds in the lid. If there was an explosion in that confined space Romana would be atomised.

The Doctor wrenched at the base of the shield-container, trying to open it, but it was firmly sealed. 'I can't move it,' he groaned. 'I can't move it!'

Through the casing, he could see the timer continuing its count-down.

There seemed to be less than thirty seconds left.

11

Stalemate

The Doctor fought desperately to free Romana from the Nova Device, his hands slipping on the smooth transparent material. Something cold touched his neck, there was an electronic buzz and he fell back unconscious.

Commander Sharrel and Agella stood looking down at him.

There was a whirr and a click from the Nova Device as the timer reached its limit. But that was all – this time there was no contained explosion.

Commander Sharrel frowned. 'A malfunction, Agella?'

'No, Commander. I did not arm the Device. Since our purpose was simply to trap the Doctor, it did not appear necessary.'

'Very well. Bring them back to the ship.'

Tyssan watched from hiding as Movellan crewman carried the Doctor, the Nova Device and the imprisoned Romana back towards their ship.

Davros was installed king-like in the control area, surrounded by his court of deferential Daleks.

'Advise Dalek central control that I require immediate transportation from this planet.'

The Dalek leader said, 'That has been done

already. A deep space cruiser is on its way.'

'When will it reach Skaro?'

'Estimated arrival time, six planetary hours.'

'Six hours?' screamed Davros. 'Too long. Every moment we stay on Skaro we are vulnerable to Movellan attack. How many Daleks remain fully operational?'

'Seven.'

Davros sighed despairingly. 'Seven! They will remain in a state of full alert until I am on board the cruiser and safely away in space, is that understood?'

'It shall be as you command.'

'*My* safety, *my* survival, are your primary concern now. You will make any sacrifice required in order to protect me!'

'We obey.'

'Very well. Now, I need to be briefed on the logistics and status of the Dalek battle fleet, and on the latest moves in this war with the Movellans.'

'We have a computersphere containing all available information. It was prepared for the Supreme Dalek.'

'Supreme Dalek?' sneered Davros. 'That is a title and status that I shall dispute when the time comes. *I* created the Daleks! I shall decide their destiny. *I* am Supreme Commander, is that clear?'

Tonelessly the Dalek leader said, 'It is understood. You will be obeyed.'

'Excellent! Now, fetch the computersphere and then leave me.'

A Dalek glided forward with a glowing transparent sphere mounted on a mobile stand. The sphere was brought close to Davros's chair and at an impatient wave of his hand, the Daleks moved away.

Davros produced an extension lead, and plugged it

into the sphere, which glowed and hummed.

He lay back in his chair, absorbing the flood of data.

Agella marched up to Commander Sharrel. 'Chargers are operating at full capacity, power-sources now running up. We will have launch capability in precisely thirty-two minutes.'

'Commence lift-off countdown!'

The Doctor and Romana, both still unconscious, were propped up in chairs nearby. Exhibiting his usual extraordinary powers of recovery, the Doctor opened his eyes and groaned.

Commander Sharrel glanced briefly at him, and then turned to Lan. 'Is the Nova Device now re-set?'

'Yes, Commander.'

'It will be safer if the Device is operated manually. If we rely on the timing device, we cannot be certain that the Daleks will not find and de-activate it. The Device must be guarded until the last possible moment. Unfortunately, the one left behind will be destroyed when he operates the Device. It is wasteful, but necessary. That will be your function, Lan.'

Lan accepted his death sentence calmly. 'Yes, Commander.'

'Take the Nova Device to the designated location. Report when you are in position. You will detonate the Device when you receive my signal.'

'Yes, Commander!' Lan lifted the Nova Device, lighter now without its protective shield, and marched away.

The Doctor sat up and rubbed his neck. 'You know, one would be deeply moved by such bravery and self-sacrifice – if one didn't know he was programmed for it and couldn't act any other way.'

'Welcome back, Doctor,' said Commander Sharrel.

'To the land of the living? It's hardly that, is it? A race of robots fighting a race of semi-robots. I knew the Universe was done for the moment they invented the washing machine.'

The Doctor leaned over to Romana and slapped her face gently. She twisted her head to and fro and groaned.

'Have no fear, Doctor, she will soon recover,' said Commander Sharrel indifferently. 'Tell me, when did you first realise that we were robotic?'

'I suspected it when you wouldn't let me see Lan's body. I was sure when the roof fell on Agella here. One hand was sticking out of the rubble. I took a look at it and saw it was regenerating itself. Humans don't mend that quickly.'

'That is so,' agreed Commander Sharrel. 'Disfunction, what humanoids call death, only occurs in us as a result of massive circuitry disturbances. We are infinitely superior to humanoids.'

'Are you now? Well, that depends on your criteria, doesn't it?'

'We function with complete logicality,' said Sharrel proudly.

'Which is why you'll never defeat the Daleks!' said the Doctor triumphantly. 'Let me demonstrate. Romana, we're going to play a game.'

'We are, Doctor?' said Romana muzzily.

The Doctor moved his chair closer to hers. 'We are. Feeling better?'

'Yes, Doctor.'

'Good. Now you remember that old Earth game I taught you?'

Davros unplugged himself from the computersphere and looked at the Daleks, who were hovering at a respectful distance. 'At last the Daleks have met a foe worthy of their powers. The Movellans, a race of robots!'

The Dalek leader moved forward. 'Dalek superiority will ultimately triumph. The Movellans will be exterminated.'

'Yet according to this report, you have been fighting them for centuries, and still you are not victorious. Two gigantic computerised battle fleets, manoeuvring in deep space. Thousands of galactic battle cruisers, vying with each other for position – for centuries – and scarcely a shot fired.'

'We shall not attack until we reach the moment of maximum advantage.'

Davros laughed sardonically. 'And neither will they! That moment will never come, for either of you. You have reached a logical impasse.'

'You will re-programme our battle computers. The Movellans will be exterminated!'

Davros's thin-lipped mouth twitched in the shadow of a smile. 'So – that is why you have returned to Skaro, to find your creator!'

'Paper,' said the Doctor, and held out an open hand.

At the same moment Romana said, 'Stone,' and held out a fist.

'Paper wraps stone,' said the Doctor triumphantly. 'I win. Again! Scissors!'

'Stone! Stone blunts scissors!' said Romana. '*I* win, Doctor.'

The Doctor turned to the astonished Movellans. 'Supposing we were two battle computers, each trying to outmanoeuvre the other, like you and the Daleks. Go on, you try it.'

'I do not see the purpose of this, Doctor.'

'*Try it!*'

Sharrel and Agella sat down to play the game. Both spoke at once. 'Stone!' The game was a draw.

'Try again!'

At exactly the same time, both said, 'Scissors.' They tried a third time. 'Paper!'

'And again!'

This time both snapped, 'Stone!'

'You see,' said the Doctor triumphantly. 'Romana and I have individual minds. Occasionally there's a draw, but mostly one or other of us wins. But you two are robots, and your minds follow logical paths – the *same* paths. So you get a draw every time. The Daleks are as good as robots too, and the same thing happens when you try to outguess them.' The Doctor laughed. 'Two of the greatest battle fleets in the Universe, caught in a logical stalemate. It sounds to me as if you've discovered the perfect formula for everlasting peace. Congratulations!'

Commander Sharrel slammed his fist upon a console. 'Our objective is not peace, Doctor. It is victory! The total destruction of the Dalek fleet!' Savagely he mimed the action of scissors cutting paper. 'Our battle computers must have some new element programmed into them, some advantage, however small, that will tip the balance in our favour.'

'That's what the Daleks want, too. That's why they came back to Skaro – to reactivate Davros.'

'We suspected something of the sort. When one Dalek scout ship broke away from the main fleet, we followed it here. It was our good fortune that we encountered you, Doctor. Romana has told us of your history, your skills. When we rejoin our fleet, *you* will re-programme our battle computers.'

'Oh, I will, will I?' said the Doctor indignantly.

'The Dalek fleet will be wiped out. Nothing will stand in the way of the Movellan conquest of the galaxy.'

'You sound just as bad as the Daleks,' said Romana. 'If not worse!'

The Doctor stood up. 'There's something you seem to have overlooked. Even if I were willing to help you change the balance of power – which I'm not, incidentally – then Davros would be attempting to do exactly the same thing for the Daleks. The man may be raving mad, but he is a fully paid up genius, and his computer skills are almost as great as mine.'

Romana smiled. 'You're too modest, Doctor.'

'I know. It's always been one of my most endearing features!'

'The problem will not arise,' said Commander Sharrel confidently. 'The moment we are in space, the Nova Device will be detonated, and this planet will fry in its own atmosphere. Davros will finally be destroyed!'

The Doctor stared at him in horror. 'But there are still dozens of Dalek prisoners on that planet. What about them?'

Commander Sharrel turned away. 'I am sorry, Doctor. In war some sacrifices are unavoidable.'

Lan sat in a rocky hollow, the Nova Device beside him, waiting patiently for the signal that would destroy a planet and end his own existence. He heard the rattle of a stone and jumped up. 'Who's there?'

There was no answer. Then he heard a groan.

Blaster in hand, Lan made his way towards the sound. On the other side of the rocks he saw Tyssan sprawled out across the path. He knelt to examine him – and another slave worker appeared in the rocks above him.

Lan whirled round, raising his blaster. Tyssan came to life, jumping up and snatching the silver tube from Lan's belt. Lan staggered about jerkily for a moment or two, and then collapsed.

Tyssan slipped the cover from the silver tube, revealing a mass of printed micro-circuits. Before his capture, Tyssan had been a very fine engineer, and robotics had been one of his specialities. He produced tools from a tattered pouch at his belt and set to work. 'Here, and here, I think,' he muttered. 'And if I reverse this circuit here . . .' He worked for a while longer, put the tube together again, and advanced on the prostrate Lan.

'Now let's see if the Doctor was right!'

An aide was delivering a report to the Dalek leader. 'Surface scanners indicate Movellan ship preparing for launch. Estimated lift-off time, twenty-one minutes. Audio scanners have detected non-Movellan voices inside space vehicle. Computers identify voice prints as Doctor and companion.'

Davros said agitatedly, 'The Doctor! The Movellans must be prevented from escaping at all costs. The

Doctor could programme Movellan battle computers as well as I could yours. He would counteract any advantage I could gain for you. The Movellans must be stopped.'

The Dalek leader said, 'Present strength will not permit open attack. Only seven Dalek units still operational.'

Davros's withered hand clenched and unclenched. 'The Movellan ship must be destroyed – at whatever cost!'

'Available fire-power will be ineffective against Movellan hull.'

'Then we must manufacture more fire-power!' Davros began wheeling up and down the control centre, ranging about restlessly as his mind grappled with the problem. He reached the rack that held the explosives and halted his chair. 'Wait! I have it! Unpack the explosives!'

12

Suicide Squad

The Movellan crew were busy with preparations for blast-off – all except the crewman who had been left to guard the Doctor and Romana, and a second guard by the door.

The two prisoners were engaged in a desultory game of 'Scissors cut paper'.

'Scissors,' said Romana, triumphantly cutting the Doctor's paper. 'You're cutting it a bit fine aren't you, Doctor? Isn't it time we got out of here?'

'Yes,' said the Doctor gloomily. 'Trouble is, I haven't the faintest idea how to go about it!'

'Well, do something – anything!'

'All right. Be ready to make a dash for it when I give the signal.' The Doctor rose and took a step towards Commander Sharrel. 'Excuse me, Commander.'

The guard put the muzzle of his blaster to the Doctor's neck. Hurriedly the Doctor sat down again.

'What happened to your plan?' whispered Romana.

'It never really got off the ground!'

'Well, we will, if you don't get a move on!'

Romana held out her hand. 'Paper!'

'Jelly baby,' said the Doctor and dropped a jelly baby into her hand.

Romana looked at it in amazement. 'Jelly baby?'

The Doctor grinned. 'Unpredictability! In other words, humanoids catch robot!'

They saw Agella move across to Commander Sharrel. 'Excuse me, Commander, I've just checked Lan's communication circuit, and he doesn't answer.'

Commander Sharrel frowned. 'It is vital that we stay in touch with him. You'd better go and check up.'

'Immediately, Commander.'

Agella moved away, and Commander Sharrel returned his attention to the flight deck. 'Commence launch programme.'

'Launch programme commencing – now!'

Agella came down the ship's ramp and saw a silver tube lying on the ground. (Although she didn't know it, this was the tube the Doctor had taken from the Movellan who had tried to capture him earlier.)

Puzzled, Agella bent to pick it up, but as she straightened up her arms were pinioned from behind. She struggled wildly, but despite her enormous robotic strength, her captor held her powerless. Agella opened her mouth to shout, but a hand came up and clamped over her mouth. With unbelieving horror, Agella saw that it was a robotic hand like her own. She was being attacked by another Movellan.

Tyssan darted from behind a rock, and snatched the silver tube from Agella's belt. Her captor released her, and she staggered a few paces and collapsed. 'Well done, Lan,' said Tyssan, and patted the Movellan on the back. He opened Agella's silver tube and began making rapid adjustments to the circuits.

Lan looked on with calm approval.

A ragged group began to appear from over the rise

– Dalek slave workers, ready to fight for their freedom.

Patiently, they waited for Tyssan to finish his task.

Davros addressed the six Daleks ranged in a semi-circle before him. 'Now, understand me clearly. You will not deviate from your task, no matter what the provocation.'

He surveyed the group. Each Dalek wore a kind of harness, a belt loaded with a double row of the canister bombs. Each of the six Daleks was now a mobile bomb of colossal power.

Davros went on. 'Let no opposition halt you. When you reach the Movellan ship, position yourself as close as possible to the hull. Then signal your arrival to me here.'

Davros paused impressively. 'Remember, the sacrifice you make now will ensure total and overwhelming Dalek victory in the war with the Movellans. Now go, and carry out your orders.'

The Daleks moved away. Only one Dalek was left in control now: the Dalek leader had been spared to act as Davros's bodyguard. All the rest were doomed, willing sacrifices to Davros's plan.

'Overwhelming Dalek victory,' repeated Davros to himself. 'Then I shall lead them on to still greater conquests. I will lead – and they will follow!'

Davros's head fell to his chest and he lay slumped in his chair, dreaming of never-ending Dalek victories.

The door had been left open when Agella went out.

The Doctor glanced up and was delighted to see Tyssan standing in the doorway. Tyssan put a finger to his lips and pointed to the Movellan who stood close to the ramp on guard. Luckily he was facing inwards, absorbed in the preparations for the launch.

Suddenly the Doctor jumped to his feet, glaring down at Romana. 'Don't you dare talk to me like that! Never say it again, do you hear me? Never!'

Romana stood up too, staring at him in astonishment. 'What did I say?'

'Jelly babies!' shouted the Doctor.

'What?'

The guards moved closer as if to separate them and the Doctor shouted, 'You keep out of this!'

The guard from the door moved over, obviously intending to assist his fellow. The Doctor turned on him. 'You too! This is a personal matter, so you mind your own business.'

Guessing the Doctor's plan, Romana joined in. 'That's right, Doctor, you tell him!'

'Keep out of this, Romana,' yelled the Doctor.

'What?'

The Doctor saw Lan and Agella appear in the doorway, blasters in their hands. 'Duck,' he yelled and threw himself to the ground dragging Romana with him.

A fierce battle raged over their heads as Lan and Agella calmly shot down their former colleagues. Ragged men clutching improvised weapons flooded into the ship, and one by one the Movellan crewmen were blasted or clubbed down.

The Doctor struggled to his feet and forced his way through the mêlée. Sitting down in Commander Sharrel's empty command chair, he flicked a series of switches and a jagged high-pitched electronic hum screamed through the control room, forcing those of the Movellans wearing headphones, and many of those who were not, to collapse in helpless agony.

The Doctor's intervention proved the turning point, and soon the remaining Movellans were subdued.

Tyssan ran up to the Doctor and Romana and there was a brief but joyful reunion.

'I don't understand,' said Romana, puzzled. 'Why were Lan and Agella helping you?'

The Doctor picked up a silver tube, snatched from a fallen Movellan. 'Because they have robot minds, like this – and a robot mind can be changed with a screwdriver – eh, Tyssan?'

Romana stared at the tube. 'That's a Movellan mind?'

'Well, not exactly a mind. It's a power pack with a number of main programming circuits.'

'I see. Orders for the day, and the energy to carry them out!'

'Something like that,' said the Doctor. 'Anyway, well done, Tyssan, old chap. Any word of Davros?'

'Nothing, Doctor.'

'I imagine the Daleks will be sending a ship to pick him up. They mustn't be allowed to get him.'

Tyssan looked round the ship. 'Well, you can see my force, Doctor. Two converted robots and a few half-starved ex-slaves. I don't know how we're going to stop a Dalek battle cruiser.'

'Neither do I,' said the Doctor. 'I think I'd better go alone.'

'No, Doctor,' protested Tyssan. 'At least let me come with you.'

The Doctor shook his head. 'I'm a dangerous person to be with, Tyssan – particularly when I don't know what I'm doing. You stay and sort this lot out. You're going to need this ship to get you home. I'll see you later, Romana!'

Romana nodded, accepting the Doctor's decision. 'Give my love to Davros!'

The Doctor disappeared down the ramp. He hurried across the rocky plain, making for the outskirts of the Dalek city. At just about the time he was climbing down the shaft, an army of bomb-carrying Daleks emerged from another city exit, heading for the Movellan space ship.

The Doctor saw no one at all on his journey to the control centre. When he entered it, the place seemed empty of Daleks.

There was only Davros, brooding alone in his wheelchair in the centre of the room.

He looked up at the sound of the Doctor's footsteps. 'Come in, Doctor, come in. I've been waiting for you.'

Cautiously the Doctor came forward. 'Thank you. I didn't expect getting in to see you would be so easy. There seems to be a singular lack of Daleks in these tunnels.'

'I'm afraid that thanks to your meddling the Dalek force has sustained a number of losses. Those few that remain are engaged in one *final* mission.'

'I see. And you're just waiting here till the rescue ship comes?'

'I do have one more small thing to do before I go, Doctor, but it will not take long.' Davros smiled. 'It seems we have both been very much in demand on Skaro, Doctor.'

The Doctor perched himself casually on an instrument console, close to Davros's chair. 'Well, it's always nice to be wanted.'

'Let us put aside our differences for a moment, Doctor, and talk simply as fellow scientists. The problem is a fascinating one, is it not, don't you agree?'

'It is indeed. Two vast computers so exactly matched, that neither one can out-think the other.'

Davros nodded. 'And as a result, two space fleets made completely powerless. You realise how the stalemate could be broken, of course, Doctor, how one side or the other could secure almost certain victory?'

'Of course.'

Davros seemed almost pleased. 'I knew you would see the solution. So simple, so obvious . . . but they will never see it. Would you have told the Movellans?'

'No.'

'I suspected as much. But I dared not take the risk. I *had* to stop the Movellans from taking you.'

'But you didn't stop them,' pointed out the Doctor. 'It was Tyssan and his escaped prisoners who set me free. They're going to use the Movellan ship to go back to Earth.'

Davros smiled triumphantly. 'I'm afraid the Movellan ship will never take off. Soon six Daleks, carrying more than a megaton of explosives between them, will press against the hull. Once they are in position I shall simply press this switch, and the bombs will detonate.'

'You can't do that! Romana and all the freed prisoners are on board now.'

'How unfortunate, Doctor,' said Davros mockingly.

The Doctor slid down from his console and took a step forward. 'And what if I decide to press that detonator-switch now – blowing up your Dalek suicide squad *before* it reaches the ship? How would you stop me?'

'I wouldn't,' said Davros, still in that mocking tone.

'I would, Doctor,' said a grating metallic voice. The Dalek leader glided forward, his gun-stick trained on the Doctor.

'You see?' said Davros softly. 'There is nothing you can do to stop it now. That ship is doomed.'

13

Blow-up

The bodies of the de-activated Movellans had been laid out in a neat row. Tyssan and his ragged crew were preparing the space ship for blast-off.

Romana walked along the row of robot bodies, looking at face after face.

Tyssan saw what she was doing and came over to her. 'What's the matter? We got them all, didn't we?'

'What about Commander Sharrel?'

'Isn't he amongst this lot?'

'I can't find him.'

'Well, it doesn't matter does it?' said Tyssan uneasily. 'I mean, even if he did get away, he can't do much on his own . . .'

'I suppose not, but . . .' Romana stopped, struck by a sudden appalling thought. 'The Nova Device. He'll try to detonate the Nova Device . . . and the Doctor's still out there. Where did you say you saw Lan with it?'

Tyssan gave rapid directions, and Romana dashed out of the ship.

Commander Sharrel had been wounded in the battle, but he was far from de-activated. He crawled slowly and determinedly across the rocks to the spot where the Nova Device waited in the niche just as Lan had left it.

Tyssan was making the final preparations for blast-off when a scout came tearing into the ship. 'Daleks! About half a dozen of them, heading this way!'

Tyssan raised his voice. 'Listen to me, all of you. The Daleks are coming to attack the ship. Pick up what weapons you can. We've got to hold them off. Remember, if any of us is ever going to get home again, we've got to save this ship!'

Snatching up Movellan blasters, the slaves headed for the ramp.

They encountered the line of advancing Daleks at the bottom of the rise. Immediately the prisoners started shooting, sending a ragged volley of blaster fire across the plain.

But the ex-prisoners were weak, half-starved, and many were civilians with no combat experience. The Daleks held together as a tightly disciplined force and swept the ranks of their attackers with a withering blast of concerted fire. Several of the prisoners screamed and fell, killed by that first terrible volley. For all Tyssan's urgings, the rest began to fall back.

Delayed rather than halted, the Daleks forged on towards the ship.

Commander Sharrel reached the Nova Device at last, and rested, gathering his failing energies. As he reached for the detonating switch, Romana leaped on him from the rocks and pulled his hand away. They fought desperately. Wounded as he was, Commander Sharrel's robotic strength was still enormous. He threw Romana to one side, and reached for the switch. Romana scrambled to her feet and launched a tremendous kick. It connected with the silver tube in Commander Sharrel's belt. He fell back, flailed wildly for a moment and then collapsed.

Grabbing the small black box that held the power to destroy a planet, Romana sat down on a handy rock, exhausted, but triumphant.

'Naturally, Doctor,' said Davros silkily, 'when the Dalek ship arrives, you will accompany me. I imagine the Daleks will consider your capture as a most welcome bonus.'

'They will undoubtedly welcome me with open arms,' said the Doctor solemnly. 'Or at least, they would· if they had them. Open suckers, shall we say . . .'

Under cover of this nonsense the Doctor was preparing to make his move. He swept off his hat and skimmed it over the eye-stalk of the watching Dalek.

Blinded, the Dalek swung helplessly to and fro.

'Behind you,' screamed Davros, and the Dalek fired.

But the Doctor had already moved on.

'To your right!' The Dalek fired again, and again it missed. A chunk of wall close to the Doctor burst into flames.

The Doctor dashed across the room and rooted in the almost empty explosives cabinet.

Only one canister bomb was left. The Doctor snatched it up. Setting the detonator switch for an immediate explosion, he triggered the bomb and lobbed it at the Dalek. It rolled along the floor, came to rest just in front of the Dalek. The bomb exploded

– and the Dalek exploded too, its casing enveloped in sheets of flame.

The Doctor walked steadily towards Davros, who retreated frantically, screaming, 'Keep back! Keep back!'

The Doctor reached out and put his hand on the detonating switch. 'My only regret is that I can't be there to see it!' He pressed the switch.

Scattering their ex-prisoners before them, the six Daleks paused at the crest of the rise, ready to hurl themselves against the Movellan ship – and exploded simultaneously in sheets of flame. The prisoners stared incredulously at the line of blazing Daleks as they blazed like strange metal beacons on the crest of the rise.

The Movellan ship was ready for take-off at last. The Doctor was saying a kind of farewell to Davros, who sat on the flight deck, surrounded by a cube-shaped construction of electronic circuitry.

For some reason the Doctor was trying to show Davros where he had gone wrong, though it was obvious to Romana at least that he was wasting his time.

'Listen,' said the Doctor. 'All elephants are pink. Nellie is an elephant. Therefore Nellie is pink. Logical?'

'Perfectly,' said Davros wearily.

'But don't you see? It's all based on a faulty first premise, so logic isn't any use to you, it's still nonsense. And do you know what a human would say to that?'

'What?'

'He'd say don't be silly, elephants aren't pink.'

'Humans do not understand logic,' said Davros scornfully.

'They understand it, but they're not slaves to it,' said the Doctor. 'Not in the way the Daleks and the Movellans are. That's why the Daleks came back for you. They remembered they'd once been organic creatures themselves, capable of intuitive, irrational, *emotional* thought. They wanted you to give those qualities back to them, to get them out of their logical trap.'

'In any event,' said Davros bleakly, 'I have failed. What will happen to me?'

It was Tyssan who answered him. 'I've already made contact with Earth. A deep space cruiser is on its way to meet us. You will be taken back to Earth and put on trial for your crimes against all sentient life-forms.'

'No deep space cruiser will hold me,' sneered Davros.

'This little device will,' said the Doctor, indicating the cubic framework. 'It's a cryogenic restraining unit. Even you can't escape from that.'

He touched a control and the air around Davros shimmered and solidified into a block of solid ice.

'Good-bye, old chap,' said the Doctor softly. 'Hope you've got your winter woollies on!'

Tyssan looked with satisfaction at the dim shape of the frozen Davros. 'You'll be needed on Earth as well, Doctor. They want you to testify at Davros's trial.'

'What?' said the Doctor indignantly. 'Spend ages standing in some stuffy courtroom?'

'You must go, Doctor. It is your duty.'

'Yes, of course,' agreed the Doctor. 'Come on, Romana, we'd better go and find our cabins.'

Tyssan was already in position on the flight deck. 'All systems running. Ready for lift-off.'

He didn't notice the Doctor and Romana slipping quietly away.

14

Departure

The Doctor and Romana were watching the ship blast off. They had shovels in their hands.

The ship rose higher, higher, until it finally disappeared into the grey clouds that hung over Skaro.

'What happens when they find out we're not on board?' asked Romana.

The Doctor grinned. 'Who cares? They'll never find us now. Come on, we've got some digging to do.'

The Doctor and Romana made their way back to the TARDIS and started digging away the rubble.

'Tell me something, Doctor,' said Romana. 'Could you really have solved the Movellans' problem and won the war for them – if you'd wanted to?'

'Of course I could.'

'How?'

'My dear girl, the answer is perfectly obvious.'

'Oh, is it?'

'Yes! Both sides were more or less robots, fighting a war directed by computers, right?'

'Right.'

'So their strategies were always perfectly logical. Each computer could predict and counter any move made by the other side. Result, stalemate.'

'Yes, I know all that, Doctor,' said Romana patiently. 'But how do you break that stalemate?'

'Oh, come on, Romana, it's very simple. If each side can predict the actions of the opposing computer, and those predictions are always based on logic – then the first side that just switches its computer off and does something illogical . . .'

'Wins the battle!'

'Exactly! Make mistakes, and confuse the enemy!'

'Brilliant. Is that why you always win, Doctor?'

'Is what why I always win?'

'Because you make so many mistakes!' said Romana innocently.

The Doctor was highly indignant, and he was still protesting that that wasn't what he'd meant at all, when the TARDIS's door was finally cleared.

He fumbled for the key. 'Make mistakes! Me?' He paused. 'Well, maybe the odd one or two, you know. Oh, say every century or so . . .'

He opened the door and they went inside.

A minute or two later there was a wheezing, groaning sound and the TARDIS dematerialised.

Almost immediately, it materialised again.

Inside the TARDIS control room Romana was saying patiently, 'No. Not that switch, Doctor – *that* one!'

'What?' said the Doctor. 'Oh yes.' He grinned at her. 'You see – that just proves what I was saying!'

The TARDIS dematerialised again, successfully this time. The Doctor and Romana were on their way to new adventures.

Δ	0426118936	Philip Hinchcliffe **DOCTOR WHO AND THE** **MASQUE OF MANDRAGORA**	70p
Δ	0426112520	Terrance Dicks **DOCTOR WHO AND THE** **PLANET OF THE DALEKS**	60p
Δ	0426106555	Terrance Dicks **DOCTOR WHO AND THE PLANET OF** **THE SPIDERS**	70p
Δ	0426200616	Terrance Dicks **DOCTOR WHO AND THE** **ROBOTS OF DEATH**	70p
Δ	042611308X	Malcolm Hulke **DOCTOR WHO AND THE** **SEA-DEVILS**	70p
Δ	0426116585	Philip Hinchcliffe **DOCTOR WHO AND THE** **SEEDS OF DOOM**	60p
Δ	0426200497	Ian Marter **DOCTOR WHO AND THE** **SONTARAN EXPERIMENT**	60p
Δ	0426110331	Malcolm Hulke **DOCTOR WHO AND THE** **SPACE WAR**	60p
Δ	0426119738	Terrance Dicks **DOCTOR WHO AND THE** **TALONS OF WENG-CHIANG**	60p
Δ	0426115007	Terrance Dicks **DOCTOR WHO AND THE** **TERROR OF THE AUTONS**	60p
Δ	0426200233	Terrance Dicks **DOCTOR WHO AND THE** **TIME WARRIOR**	60p
Δ	0426113241	Bill Strutton **DOCTOR WHO AND THE ZARBI (illus)**	70p
Δ	0426200012	Terrance Dicks **THE SECOND DOCTOR WHO** **MONSTER BOOK (Colour illus)**	70p
	0426118421	Terrance Dicks **DOCTOR WHO DINOSAUR BOOK**	75p
	0426116151	Terrance Dicks and Malcolm Hulke **THE MAKING OF DOCTOR WHO**	60p
	0426200020	**DOCTOR WHO DISCOVERS** **PREHISTORIC ANIMALS (NF) (illus)**	75p

†For sale in Britain and Ireland only.
*Not for sale in Canada.
◆ Film & T.V. tie-ins.

If you enjoyed this book and would like to have information sent to you about other TARGET titles, write to the address below.

You will also receive:
A FREE TARGET BADGE!
Based on the TARGET BOOKS symbol — see front cover of this book — this attractive three-colour badge, pinned to your blazer-lapel or jumper, will excite the interest and comment of all your friends!

and you will be further entitled to:
FREE ENTRY INTO THE TARGET DRAW!
All you have to do is cut off the coupon below, write on it your name and address in *block capitals,* and pin it to your letter. Twice a year, in June, and December, coupons will be drawn 'from the hat' and the winner will receive a complete year's set of TARGET books.

Write to:

TARGET BOOKS
44 Hill Street
London W1X 8LB

cut here

Full name ....

Address...

....

....

Age......................

PLEASE ENCLOSE A SELF-ADDRESSED STAMPED ENVELOPE WITH YOUR COUPON!